TEXAS FRIDAYS

HOUSTON

SAM MOUSSAVI

EPIC
Press

Houston
Texas Fridays

Written by Sam Moussavi

Published by EPIC Press™
PO Box 398166
Minneapolis, MN 55439

Cover design by Kali Yeado
Images for cover art obtained from iStockPhoto.com
Edited by Gil Conrad

LIBRARY OF CONGRESS CATALOGING-IN-PUBLICATION DATA

Names: Moussavi, Sam, author.
Title: Houston / by Sam Moussavi.
Description: Minneapolis, MN : EPIC Press, 2017. | Series: Texas Fridays
Summary: Darren Taylor is a defensive end, and before his senior season, his biggest issue was
    deciding where to go to college. But a painful injury leads to drug addiction, and threatens
    to derail Darren's hope of getting away from his tough neighborhood in Houston's Third
    Ward.
Identifiers: LCCN 2016946142 | ISBN 9781680764949 (lib. bdg.) |
    ISBN 9781680765502 (ebook)
Subjects: LCSH: High school—Fiction. | Football—Fiction. | Football players—Fiction. |
    Drug abuse—Fiction. | Inner cities—Fiction. | Life change events—Fiction. | Young adult
    fiction.
Classification: DDC [Fic]—dc23
LC record available at http://lccn.loc.gov/2016946142

For those eager to take liberties with the imagination and stay awhile.

—Pete Simonelli

1

"IT'S ABOUT RESPECT, DARREN," MARQUIS SAID.

Darren's older brother, Marquis, was all about respect. Darren had heard this speech before, and many others that sounded something close to it.

"That's why when someone comes at me," Marquis said, racking a bullet into a nine-millimeter pistol, "*I* finish it. Remember *this* game is all about respect."

Marquis and Darren Taylor were well known in the Third Ward section of southeast Houston, albeit for two different reasons. Darren was a football star, an All-State defensive end, entering his senior season at KIPP Sunnyside High School in the Third Ward.

"You know what KIPP stands for, right?" Marquis asked, lowering the gun.

"Nah," Darren said.

"You don't know what the name of your school means? KIPP. Knowledge Is Power Program."

"For real?"

"Keep getting it on the football field, Darren" Marquis said. "But make sure you leave time to get a little something from the classroom too."

Darren looked into his older brother's eyes. They were black, but not like the edge of darkness. Marquis's eyes didn't remind Darren of death, pain, or exploitation. They were a soft black. The truth was, they made Darren feel safe.

"*This* is power," Marquis said, lifting the nine millimeter again. "But there are other kinds of power, too."

Darren knew deep down inside that the more violent part of his brother's speech was not true. He always knew that being out on the corner was wrong. He was lucky that football gave him an outlet. A lot of Darren's boys did not have the opportunity he had because he could play a game. Football would be his ticket out of the Third Ward—the place that would always be home—and though he'd miss his brothers and his boys, Darren had to get out.

"Come on. I'll drop you off at school," Marquis said, placing the pistol in the waistband of his sagging jeans. He draped his white, double-XL t-shirt over the gun. "You're late as it is."

They got into Marquis's black Ford Expedition. The ride sat on chrome twenty-twos. Marquis wanted to tint the windows to high hell, but he knew better. The cops around the Third Ward knew him well. Marquis was not about to give the police a silly scent to sniff around. Not with all he had at stake. If Marquis was going down, he wanted it to mean something.

They drove past the old, decrepit church on the corner, the old Shell gas station, and finally, Milt's Liquor Store—which was always open bright and early, rain or shine.

"I lost another soldier last night," Marquis said.

Darren was focused on what was going on outside the window.

"Are you hearing me?" Marquis said, with a backhand to Darren's chest.

"Yeah. What's up?"

"What's going on, up there?" Marquis asked as he tapped the side of his brother's head. "You're not focused. You're somewhere else all the time."

"Yo, let me ask you something."

"Hit me."

"Where do you see yourself, in like, five, ten years?"

Marquis put a couple of fingers to the fuzz he had growing on his chin. A curious smile peeled onto his face. "I don't see anything. The way I live my life. A nigga can't see that."

"Yeah, but this can't be it," Darren said, waving a hand at the passing Third Ward behind the glass.

"This is all I know, little brother," Marquis said

Darren watched his older brother in silence.

Marquis paused and held a faraway look before snapping back.

"But the way I live," Marquis continued, "it ain't for you."

2

DARREN SHOOK IT OFF BEFORE WALKING THROUGH the threshold and into the halls of Sunnyside High. He passed by a few of the girls who liked him—or so he'd heard through the grapevine—but he didn't give them the time. He liked to play it cool with females, something else he had picked up from his older brother. According to Marquis, there was no good that could come from playing it any other way with the opposite sex.

Before homeroom, he took a detour to the cafeteria to pick up breakfast. With Marquis around that morning, it had slipped Darren's mind to grab something to eat on the way out. Sunnyside, like many other schools that operated in low-income areas, had a program that provided a free, hot breakfast for those who couldn't get one at home. Darren didn't fall under the category of needy as Marquis always had the fridge and pantries stocked at the house.

First period was U.S. Government, and the class was filled with uninterested football players. Most of them slept while the newbie teacher—sent into the Third Ward by Teach for America—stood at the head of the class lecturing his heart out. Darren sometimes slept through first period and sometimes didn't. One thing he never did was listen. To him, the U.S. government meant nothing, and its prime enforcers—the cops—were just out there to make life hard for a nigga trying to come up.

For the most part, Darren agreed with his older brother's view of how the system worked. He had seen Marquis being hassled by the local Third Ward rollers—the uniformed cops—or the "knockos"—the ones in plainclothes. He had all the evidence he needed to know that what his brother told him was true. As a result, Darren spent his time in all of his classes thinking about football. That was the only reason he was there in the first place. If it weren't for football, he'd be out in the Third Ward, alongside Marquis and his boys, putting stuff out into the streets and getting stuff done. School was a one-way path. It wasn't like he'd go to college without football.

There was a tap on Darren's shoulder from behind. "Yo," a voice said.

Darren turned to see who was behind him. The voice belonged to Dez, a starting cornerback on the team.

"What's good?" Darren asked, as they shook.

The teacher engaged in a dialogue with a couple of students in the front of the class, who were making eye contact with him.

"Shorty-Boy got hit last night," Dez said. Dez was also from the Third Ward and had a brother in the game. He also used football as insurance against the corners. "Your brother is probably heated."

Darren remembered that Marquis had mentioned something in the car. That there would be trouble the next few days and nights around the neighborhood. Marquis hadn't mentioned Shorty-Boy by name, however.

"They know who did it?" Darren asked.

"Nah, not yet," Dez said. "Probably them two-eight-one niggas."

"Damn," Darren said.

"What?"

"Gonna be trouble."

"Yeah, this ain't no joke. Shorty-Boy had respect."

Darren shook his head and turned back around. He closed his eyes and wished that three o'clock would come. He wished he could fast-forward through the rest of the school day. There was nothing for him in class, and the rest of the day would be filled with gossip about what his brother was going to do when he found Shorty-Boy's killer. Darren *needed* to get out of the classroom and onto the field.

"I'm just letting you niggas know right now," Dez proclaimed to a group of teammates before practice. "It's not a game. This here is life and death. Don't go reppin' the wrong block, or you might end up blasted."

Darren turned a deaf ear to Dez's pre-practice mess. That stuff meant something to the wide-eyed, approval-seeking underclassmen who looked up to Dez, but not for anyone who knew any better. Darren and Dez were from the same neighborhood, and both played football. But that's where the comparison ended. Unlike Dez, Darren didn't *act* like he was in the drug game. Dez, on the other hand, liked to front that he was a player. Marquis had told Darren about a situation that summer past when Dez's older brother, Mike, tried to help Dez earn some money. Mike came to Marquis with a proposal, and Marquis agreed to front Dez a package. Trouble was, Dez had no credibility out on the corner. That combined with his lack of experience, led to a series of broken promises and flat-out refusals to pay, rendering the package a financial sinkhole, rather than the windfall it should have been. When it came time for Marquis to collect, Mike had to step in for his little brother. Out of respect to Mike and their history, Marquis allowed Mike to collect the debt—and collect Mike did, with the prerequisite, revenge-soaked violence—but also cautioned that Dez would never get his hands on anymore drugs.

Dez had no idea that Darren knew this about him.

The individual portion of practice began, and both the offensive and defensive linemen went to the west end zone for one-on-ones.

During the drill, Darren made it clear why he was All-State defensive end by using a variety of moves to break through the offensive line. When the offensive tackle set hard, Darren first threw him off balance with an in-and-out fake and then used a swim move to come back inside. When the tackle's sloppy footwork left an unstable base, Darren went with a bull rush. He did not have to think about these things when he was on the field. He was gifted enough to simply do them—and *that*, according to Coach Adams, was why Darren was a special player.

Darren sustained his intensity all the way through practice and even raised it a notch during the end of practice scrimmage. He lived in the offensive back-field, and if he were allowed to hit the quarterback during the scrimmage, he would've sacked him on the first three plays. Darren was such a game—and practice—wrecker, that Coach Adams had to take him out of the scrimmage after just seven plays. Sunnyside's offense had to get something out of the practice too.

Darren watched from the sideline, next to Coach Adams.

Practice ended and the team walked toward the locker room in a large herd. Dez caught up with Darren and they walked inside together.

"I couldn't concentrate out there," Dez said.

"Why?" Darren asked.

"Shorty-Boy."

"You got nothing to do with that, Dez. Just make sure your head is in this right here. Make sure you don't get burnt in tomorrow night's scrimmage."

"We can't be lettin' niggas come into the Third Ward and kill our soldiers, can we?"

Darren thought about Dez and the package last summer. He wanted to let Dez have the truth, but decided to let it go. The truth wouldn't change Dez anyway.

"Just let Marquis and Mike take care of it," Darren said in a commanding way.

They entered the locker room, and Darren stopped in front of his locker and tossed his helmet into it.

Dez took a deep breath. "You right," he said.

They shook hands. Dez walked over to his locker, and Darren changed out of his practice gear and into shorts and a t-shirt before walking toward Coach Adams's door.

"Take a seat, Darren," Adams said.

"What's up, Coach?"

"Two Division-One teams are very interested in you. The offer letters came in today."

"Please tell me that USC is one of them."

Coach Adams nodded his head slowly. His eyes were lit up so brightly that you would think he was the one who had the scholarship offer to play big-time college ball.

"What's the other?"

"Boise State," Adams said.

"Oh yeah," Darren said. "But I'm all over USC, Coach. A nigga—" He stopped himself. "I mean, a dude like me can't wait to get out to Cali."

"I get that," Coach Adams said. "But keep Boise State in play too. That's a fantastic school up there, a solid program. And it's quiet. Maybe you could benefit from someplace low-key like that."

"Not too quiet though," Darren said with a mischievous smile.

Adams sighed. He knew Darren's upbringing, which resembled that of many other players across the seasons. It was a difficult thing to do, selling schools that were fixed in rural settings, direct opposites to the USCs of the world. The sell was particularly hard to make to inner-city Houston kids, such as Darren. But Adams believed in his pitch, and he'd give it the same way until he stopped coaching.

"Just keep them both open is what I'm saying," Adams said. "You still have plenty of time before signing day. The offers are in, that's all. And more will come."

"A'ight," Darren said. "Thanks Coach."

They shook hands, and Darren left the office.

3

To Darren's surprise, Marquis's Expedition was idling out in the back parking lot. Rides to school were no big thing. Rides home from school were rare.

Darren opened the passenger door with questioning eyes.

"Get in," Marquis said.

Darren got in and closed the door. The car was silent for the first few minutes of the ride.

"I thought this is your busy time?" Darren asked.

"It is. Just don't want nothin' stupid happening, is all," Marquis fired back.

"This about Shorty-Boy?"

Marquis looked over at Darren. It was the look that had a little bit of anger in it, along with a little bit of something close to guilt. "We gonna hit them back," Marquis said. "Plan's in motion right now."

"War?"

"Nah. No war. Where you get a word like that? It's just, they hit one of ours, so we gotta come back on them."

"And I'm at risk?"

"No, I just want to avoid something stupid happening, like I said."

"Like what?"

"Anything."

"So?" Darren persisted.

"So, the next few days, maybe a week, I'll drop you off and pick you up from school."

Darren eyed his older brother with something close to contempt.

"Just until we do what needs doing and all this blows over."

"Well, I have a scrimmage tomorrow night against Houston Christian."

"Yeah. I know. I'm gonna try to be there."

The ride was silent again. Marquis hated that word *war* as a way of describing what he and his crew engaged in when it was time to get violent. To Marquis, it wasn't that heavy. A war was something planned and carried out by people who weren't actually fighting. His thing wasn't like that at all. And though Marquis was the leader of his crew, he was still visible in the Third Ward. He didn't want to be one of these players who made all the money and hid from the police and feds, or worst of all, his people. The game was out there to be played, and when it was time to get dirty, Marquis wanted everyone in his crew to know that he wasn't above any of it.

"How's it going out there?" Marquis asked, with his eyes on the road. "On the field."

"I got it on lock. That's how it's going."

"Don't be too cocky. There's always someone coming to knock the crown off your head, put it on his own." Marquis pulled up in front of his mother's house and put the truck in park.

Darren unfastened his seatbelt. "You coming?"

Marquis scratched at his chin. "Nah, got somewhere to be. You got food in the house?"

"Yeah," Darren said. He waited for his older brother to say something, but Marquis stayed quiet. "It's about to get crazy out here, isn't it?"

Marquis shook his head. "Nah."

"Be careful."

"I'll be around in the a.m.to take you to school. Don't leave the house next couple of nights."

The two brothers shook hands, and Darren got out. He watched as Marquis pulled away and turned at the end of the street then walked inside his house. The television was turned up loud with no one there to watch, as usual. He walked over to turn down the volume, and the smell of Newports was so potent that he coughed to clear out his lungs.

"Mom!" Darren called out.

There was no response.

Darren walked upstairs and knocked lightly on his mother's bedroom door. He turned the knob and walked in to see her asleep in bed. The light was on. She wore the outfit that she had on the day before and was resting on top of the covers. An open can of beer sat on the nightstand next to the bed. The blaring television should've given it away straight off, but Darren checked on her anyway, bracing for the worst. He grabbed the can of beer off the nightstand and turned off the light.

The fridge housed leftovers from the night before—a half-chicken and a couple scoops of collards—that Darren warmed in the microwave. As he waited for his dinner, he dug out a brochure from USC that was within a pile of mail on the kitchen table. The pictures in the brochure seemed almost unreal to Darren.

All of the USC students in the brochure looked happy. Too happy. And the sun was shining in every one of the pictures. Darren had to close the brochure halfway through his meal because its content caused his mind to race. *What if I'm not as happy as all those smiling students in the pictures?*

He finished eating and put his dishes in the dishwasher. Darren took the brochure up to his room and placed it on his nightstand. With his day almost through, he took a deep breath as he sat on the edge of his bed. He closed the window and turned on the air conditioner—a window unit Marquis had installed in Darren's room.

He let the cool air fill the room and stretched out on his bed. His eyes closed and he slipped into that pocket right before sleep. That's when he heard the pops in the distance outside the closed window. He had just missed falling asleep. A few minutes later, the sirens came and inched closer, until finally, they made it into the Third Ward. Darren couldn't fall asleep for the rest of the night.

4

WHEN DARREN GOT HIMSELF UP EARLY THE NEXT morning, his mother was still asleep. Other than checking that she was breathing, he did not want to disturb her. He made himself a breakfast of honey toast and orange juice before walking out the front door at the beck and call of a car horn. A car he had never seen before was waiting outside, but Darren did not bat an eye. He'd gotten countless rides from Marquis over the years, often when his brother drove unfamiliar vehicles. When Darren opened the foreign car's passenger door, he didn't see Marquis in the driver's seat, however. Dez's older brother Mike sat there instead. He eyed Darren coolly as Darren inspected him.

"What?" Darren said. "Where's 'Quis? He ain't . . . ?"

"Nah, get in," Mike said.

"For real, Mike. I need to know. Where is my brother?"

"He's bunkered up," Mike said. "He's okay."

Darren got into the car, but not because he was through asking questions. "I wanna go see him, Mike."

Mike reached down to the cupholder in the center console and brought up a tall, styrofoam to-go cup. He drank from it deeply and then looked straight ahead as he pulled away from Darren's house.

"Take me to go see my brother, nigga," Darren demanded.

Mike pressed on the brakes, and the car squealed to a stop in the middle of the road. Two cars passed on the left, but not before hurling a few choice words in Mike's direction first.

"Stop telling me what *I* need to do, Darren. You need to calm down and listen," Mike said. Though his words were sure, his tone and demeanor were tranquilized. "It's too dangerous right now to see him. I'm here to take you to school. Marquis is safe. You have my word."

"Y'all hit back last night?"

Mike continued staring ahead.

Darren pulled out his cell phone and dialed his brother. It rang once before a robotic voice told him that the number has been disconnected.

"You ain't gonna get him on his number," Mike explained. "He's on a burner right now. No known numbers."

"What's the number?"

"Can't tell you right now. It's not safe."

"Tell my brother to call me on my cell. I need to know that he's good."

Mike was a person who did not appreciate being pressed, even by Darren, his boss's little brother. Mike took another hearty sip from his tall to-go cup, its contents keeping him mellow and his temper in check. He replaced the cup in the holder and licked the sick-sweet residue from his lips.

"You need to listen to what I'm saying to you right now. It's too hot for him to reach out. When the beef cools, he'll get at you. But until then, this is the reality, D."

Darren put his phone away and sighed.

"How's the team doing?" Mike asked. "I hear you're tearing it up out there."

"Is Marquis coming to my scrimmage tonight?"

"He can't make it tonight. He told me to tell you that he's sorry."

Darren slumped down into the seat and looked out the window. Sure enough, the Third Ward's corners were empty.

"You know he'd kill to be there."

Darren turned back to Mike. "After my scrimmage tonight, I want to go see my brother. Will you pick me up and take me to go see him? Can you do that for me?"

There was a tightness in Mike's temples that was due to all the pressure he'd faced in the last twenty-four hours. The night before was a long one and now this. Mike had his own little brother to worry about and didn't need the added responsibility of looking after Marquis's as well. But what could he do? Say no to Marquis?

He took three more baby sips. "I'll talk to 'Quis, a'ight?" Mike said, as they pulled up to the front of Sunnyside High. "Just be cool and do your thing out there tonight. I'll scoop you up after and see about taking you to Marquis."

"Thanks," Darren said before getting out of the car and slamming the passenger door shut.

. . . .

Mike pulled away from the school, leaving a little rubber on the road. He stopped the car after a few blocks and pulled over to the curb. His nerves were all over the place with all that was going on, and the only reliable thing to bring him down after killing two young men the night before was the lean in his tall, Styrofoam cup. He cut the engine and rubbed at both of his temples with the pads of his pointer fingers. The circular motions brought a temporary release of pressure, but not enough to alleviate the pinpoint jabs of pain in his skull. He finished what was in the to-go cup and placed it back in the holder with a rattle of ice.

He started the car back up and went on his way, back into the heart of the Third Ward. He took a left onto Alabama Street, and soon he was parked in front of an old house right underneath the Eastex Freeway overpass.

Marquis was inside.

Mike got out and checked to see if he had been followed. When satisfied, he opened the gate and took the walkway to the front door of the house. The door was brand new, as were the locks. He took out a set of keys, unlocked the dead-bolt, and opened the door.

Inside, the house was dark. Mike could hear a video game being played in the back. He walked through the hallway that led to the back of the house. On the way, Mike stopped in the kitchen to grab a few things. He opened one of the kitchen cabinets and picked out a brown bottle of cough syrup, among many other bottles that looked the same. The bottle was empty and after he discarded it, he sifted through the rest of the bottles until he found one at the back of the cabinet. The bottle he chose was not filled with just any over-the-counter cough suppressant. No, this stuff was the real thing—the Actavis brand—that you could only get with a prescription or a connection. Next, he filled another tall, to-go cup with ice, up to the brim. A two-liter of lemon-lime soda was then spiked with the entire brown bottle of codeine-promethzine nectar. He filled the Styrofoam cup with the blueish-purple mix from the soda bottle, and for good measure, unwrapped a few Jolly Ranchers candies, and popped them into the cup as well. With his "lean" concocted, Mike took a good sip from the to-go cup, and let the warmth wash over him. He exhaled and continued on to the back of the house.

Only he, Marquis, and a few chosen enforcers knew the location of this safe house. That was the reason Marquis showed no surprise or emotion when Mike walked into the back room. He simply nodded and Mike did the same.

"He good?" Marquis asked.

"Yeah. He's in school."

Another nod before Marquis turned his attention back to the video game, the latest offering from John Madden. Marquis was sitting on the couch and playing against the computer. There was no muscle there with him. He had sent one of them out on a food run, and the other three were posted up outside the house in watchdog positions.

Mike sat down on the couch.

"I heard you walk in like five minutes ago. What took you so long to get back here?"

Mike lifted his to-go cup and rattled the ice inside as his response.

"Oh," Marquis said.

Mike took another few sips.

Marquis placed a watchful eye on his friend, though he masked it by continuing with the video game.

"What's the plan?" Marquis asked as he fake-toggled his controller.

"Wait until night and hit that mob over on Elgin and Dowling."

"They over there by Emancipation Park, right?"

Mike nodded and took another sip.

Marquis paused the game and put the controller down on the coffee table, next to his nine-millimeter. "What did Darren say?"

"He wants to see you."

"What did you say?"

"Told him it was too hot right now. That he had to wait for you to contact him."

"You did the right thing."

"After we hit these boys tonight, it should be over."

"Those ones last night were young," Marquis said.

Mike took another sip and finally put his cup down on the coffee table. He closed his eyes and rubbed his face. He was all the way relaxed now. "I know."

"Yo, Mike, you've been sippin' hard on that drank since late last night. Don't you think you wanna cool out a little?"

"Purple drank" was another name for the lean in Mike's cup. There were many other names too: "syrup," "sizzurp," "oil," and "Texas tea." Whatever the tag, Marquis's interest in what was *in* Mike's cup brought on a series of more self-conscious sips.

"I'm straight," Mike said. "I got it under control. I just need a little somethin' to smooth it out, from all the heaviness last night. You know?"

Marquis wasn't convinced; he'd seen what lean had done to countless residents of the Third Ward over the years. He could also see where Mike was coming from in terms of needing something to calm the nerves after committing violence. Marquis himself didn't drink lean or alcohol and didn't use drugs. The violence affected people in different ways.

"We'll make sure to finish this tonight. I don't want to spend anymore nights here than I have to."

Mike nodded and stood up.

"Where you going?" Marquis asked. "The food's coming."

"I know. I just . . . I just got this headache. I'm gonna go lie down a little."

"A'ight."

Mike left the back room and walked through the hallway toward the front door. He went upstairs for a nap. The night before was a rough one for Mike. All this killing was starting to take its toll. He was in the game to make money, and that was it. All this other stuff, he wasn't so sure about anymore. He took a few more sips from his Styrofoam cup before knocking out on one of the twin beds in a bedroom upstairs.

Marquis continued his video game. The night before had been tough on him too. It wasn't the actual killing that bothered Marquis. It was that these boys were so young nowadays. The two he and Mike got the night before couldn't have been older than fifteen. Marquis couldn't look at the bodies after because they reminded him of his brother Darren. But by the time he and Mike got back to the car, the rationalizations in his head began. They were all variations on *this is the game and these are the rules.*

5

DEZ WAS DRESSED FOR THE SCRIMMAGE; HIS CLEATS and gloves were brand new out of the plastic, just as he preferred. His older brother Mike had outfitted him with pairs of new cleats and gloves for every game that season, including the scrimmage against Houston Christian. Dez sat in front of his locker, bobbing his head to the Bun-B playing in his headphones. The locker room was quiet, just like it would be on a real game day. Darren dressed at his locker, and eyed Dez as he did so.

Dez caught Darren's glance and replied with a questioning look. Darren lowered his eyes and continued getting dressed. Dez took off his headphones and walked over to Darren's locker. By the time Darren lifted his head, Dez was right next to him.

"Everything a'ight?"

"I saw your brother this morning," Darren said, pulling up his socks.

"What's up?"

"You don't know?"

"I haven't seen my brother in days," Dez said.

"They're going all out," Darren said. "I asked Mike to take me to see Marquis, but he said it wasn't safe."

"How did Mike look to you?"

"What do you mean?"

"I mean, were his eyes red? Was he rubbing his head like this?"

Dez rubbed both temples as an example.

"Nah, man," Darren said, "he *looked* fine. I don't care how your brother looks. I'm trying to find out if my brother is okay."

"I'm just asking," Dez said. "Chill."

"Mike is gonna pick me up after the scrimmage. Take me to see Marquis."

"I'm going with you."

Darren shook his head. "You need to take that up with Mike. I'm going to see my brother after the scrimmage. That's all I know."

Dez went back to his locker and grabbed his helmet. He went out to the field to warm up before anyone else on the team. Darren finished getting dressed, and with a moment to relax, took a seat in front of his locker. He looked around and saw the faces of his teammates. He didn't want to let them down with distracted play because they were his brothers, as well.

. . . .

Sunnyside held an annual joint practice and scrimmage with a private school, Houston Christian, before the start of the regular season. Houston Christian had a reputation for sending players to the best colleges in

Texas, but Darren wasn't intimidated by the school's prestige.

As he stretched, he visualized getting into the backfield and killing Houston Christian's quarterback. Not really killing him—just hitting him so hard that it affected his play for the rest of the scrimmage. That was Darren's job after all, and he liked to play angry. Releasing frustrations out on the field helped him stay calm when he was off it. He didn't know where he would be without the game.

The joint practice began with individual drills. Darren and his fellow defensive linemen went over to one end zone along with Houston Christian's offensive line. The first drill consisted of one-on-ones. Darren went first against HC's best offensive tackle, Hep Nolan. Nolan was a five-star recruit who had sewn up a scholarship to the University of Alabama with his road-grating play as a junior the season before. Coach Adams made sure not to miss the confrontation between Darren and Nolan.

Darren got down into his stance and stared at the

hulking lineman in front of him. Nolan's face was pointed downwards.

The whistle blew and the pads popped. Darren stunned Nolan, knocking him back on his heels with a two-fisted jolt. By the time Nolan recovered, it was too late. Darren bull-rushed him into the back of the end zone. A second whistle saved the stymied tackle from colliding into the goalpost. Darren didn't boast; he simply ran to the back of the line.

Coach Adams was there waiting for him with a pat on the back of helmet. "That's an All-State offensive tackle that you just made candy off," he said at a low volume, adhering to the etiquette of a joint-practice.

Inside, Coach Adams simmered with the possibilities. "We're gonna line you up inside this season. Offenses aren't gonna be able to adjust to your moving around the d-line."

"Line me up anywhere. I just want to get to the QB."

On the other end of the field, Dez and the DBs were practicing against HC's wide receivers. Just like

Darren, Dez went first in his drill, but didn't experience the same success. Better put, Dez was burnt on his first rep. He bit horribly on a double-move from HC's best receiver. If the play had occurred during a real game, it would have been an eighty-yard touchdown. Dez complained to Coach Martin, Sunnyside's DBs' coach, that Houston Christian was using "punk-ass double moves."

Martin didn't give in to Dez, telling him simply to keep quiet and get to the back of the line. During Dez's second rep, he exhibited a penchant for resiliency by playing his technique the way it was taught. Instead of going for the interception, he read the receiver and broke up the pass. Coach Adams witnessed both of Dez's reps, and after the second one, pulled the cornerback off to the side of the drill.

"You see?" Adams pleaded. "You see what happens when you play the way we teach?"

Dez nodded.

"You gotta trust what we're teaching you. If you do, you can go as far as you want to."

The next drill for Darren's group was nine-on-seven—a drill that pitted Houston Christian's offense, minus its receivers, against Sunnyside's defense, minus its defensive backs. Throwing passes was not permitted during nine-on-seven, as the drill was meant to instill physical toughness. Instead, the focus was on either running the ball or stopping the run, depending on the side.

Darren lined up at his right defensive end spot and waited for HC's offense to break the huddle. If there was any improvement that Darren had to make, it was being better against the run. During junior year, a few of the bigger teams in Sunnyside's section found success running the ball right at Darren. He aimed to neutralize this tactic by getting stronger and playing with sounder technique.

When the offense approached, HC's quarterback barked out his calls and, on the snap, turned to hand the ball off to the running back on a lead play to the left. The play came right at Darren. He rammed his inside shoulder into HC's tackle, Nolan, and forced the running back to bounce it outside. Darren's initial effort would enable the outside linebacker to come up and make the tackle. A simple play, but Darren wasn't finished yet. He shed Nolan with his off arm and pursued the running back. Just as the back reached the line of scrimmage, Darren clipped the his legs, thus, bringing the ballcarrier to the ground. *This* was the kind of play that made Darren special. The combination of power, speed and effort had Darren on his way out of the Third Ward.

Adams was the first to congratulate Darren on the play. He had believed in Darren before anyone else on Sunnyside's staff. Because of who Darren's brother was, the assumption was that Darren would be trouble as well, but Adams's mind didn't operate that way. He gave Darren a fair chance from the start. He wanted to know who *Darren* was.

Darren smiled at Coach Adams and went back to the defensive huddle. *This* is where he belonged. All of the other stuff—the streets, his brother's business—that wasn't for him.

The second play of nine-on-seven was even more impressive. HC ran a sweep away from Darren's side. Darren raced down the line of scrimmage and tracked down the running back for a loss of three. If teams could not run at Darren or away from him, Sunnyside's defense was going to be a menace.

After nine-on-seven, the head coaches on each side took their teams to opposite end zones. The scrimmage was next, but first, the two squads were afforded a chance to cool down and get water. The humidity had kicked in right before the drills began, and both sides were gassed. Darren took a water bottle and got down on one knee. Dez came over and took a knee next to him.

"Let me see that when you're through," Dez said, chin nodding toward the water bottle in Darren's big right paw.

Darren shook his head. "Get your own. It's *hot* out here."

He squirted some of the ice cold water down between his shoulder pads and back. The shock of the water hitting his skin was immediate, even though the humid air swallowed up the sensation before it even had a chance to linger.

"Yeah," Dez said. "You should have seen them over there." Dez tilted his head down to the opposite end zone where Houston Christian was. "Their receivers is straight trash."

"Is that why you got burnt on the first damn rep?" Darren asked with a smile, but also with harsh emphasis on the word 'burnt.'

"Dude pulled a double move!" Dez cried. "On the first play of the scrimmage! That's weak and you know it."

"So what?" Darren said. "I get double and triple-teamed on every play. I'm still out here doing my job."

"I straight shut them down after that first play, though."

"Aw, shut your ass up. I'm tired of hearing your mouth."

When Darren rose up, Dez did the same, looking

Darren right in the eye. "Yo, Darren. Why you playin' me like this? You been on my case all day."

Darren took a step at Dez and shoved him to the ground. When Dez hit, the rest of the team took notice. A few pockets here and there began to laugh. Dez couldn't let it ride, not with everyone on the team watching. He jumped to his feet and went back at Darren. He took a swipe and grazed the side of Darren's face. Darren locked him up in a bear hug, and that was the end of it.

"Hey!" Coach Adams yelled from behind. He pried Darren and Dez apart, and then stared at each of them wildly. Down on the other end of the field, Houston Christian had started to notice. Coach Adams managed to compose himself and kept his voice low.

"What the hell is going on with you two?" he asked through gnashed teeth. "You guys are leaders. Friends, right? What is this?"

Neither Darren nor Dez said anything. Adams put his hands on his hips like he always did when trying to solve a problem. "You guys put this to bed now," he said. "We have another team here. They can't see us fighting each other like this."

Darren and Dez slowed their breathing.

"Shake," Adams said.

. . . .

Sunnyside started the scrimmage on offense a few minutes later. The offense struggled to move the ball against Houston Christian's defense. On the third snap, Sunnyside threw an interception, and Darren strapped on his helmet.

On Houston Christian's first snap, Darren knifed into the backfield and dropped the running back for a loss of five.

HC's quarterback dropped back to pass on the second play. Darren rushed from the left side this time and, after fighting through a double team, he hit the QB just as he released the pass. The ball sailed high.

Darren made every other member of Sunnyside's defense a better player. He covered up for an inconsistent secondary—one that as a unit liked to gamble—because of how quickly he pressured the quarterback. He helped his fellow defensive linemen succeed in their matchups because they could go one-on-one. He also made the lives of his defensive coaches easier because they could devise game plans that covered up the unit's weaknesses.

On third down, HC's left tackle, Nolan, set up quickly in a pass-blocking stance. As Darren began his attack, Nolan lunged at his knees. Darren's instincts kicked in, and an alert of "screen pass!" rang in his ears. He avoided the cut block by lunging backwards. In one motion, he jumped up and extended his arms as high as they could go. Darren tipped the pass into the air, looked up to locate the ball, ran underneath it, and cradled it for the interception. Then he took it to the house, outrunning every player in pursuit.

Darren's teammates were shocked, not because of his freakish athleticism and hyperawareness, but more so by his demeanor after making a play of that nature. Darren did not celebrate after the ridiculous pick-six. He simply ran back to the sideline, slapped a few high-fives, and grabbed a drink of water.

When the buzz from the play wore off on the sideline, Darren stood there alone, taking small sips of water, while gathering his breath close in his chest. With a break from the action, he stole a hope that his brother really was alive.

. . . .

Coach Adams pulled Darren out for the next two defensive series. He knew what he had in his best player. He needed to see what the other guys could do. Plus, he had this funny feeling. He didn't want to tempt the football gods by leaving Darren out there too long in a scrimmage. It was probably just a false alarm, but Coach Adams didn't want to press it.

Darren wasn't happy to be standing on the sidelines. He hated being on the bench, especially on a day when he needed something to take his mind off Marquis—that something was football. Standing there with nothing to do, he couldn't help but dwell on his older brother. Darren walked over to Coach Adams as Sunnyside's offense was on the field.

"Ready to get me back in there?" Darren asked.

Coach Adams knew it was coming. "Just trying to get a look at some other players, Darren."

"Please Coach, I want to get back in there."

"I know you do," he said. "But think about the season. Our first game is in three weeks. Be patient. Keeping you healthy for when it counts is what's important."

"One more drive, Coach."

Coach Adams looked down to the ground briefly and then back to Darren.

"One more drive," he said. "I don't want you bugging me after that."

Darren smiled. "A'ight."

He ran onto the field as Houston Christian's offense was huddled up. He lined up in his normal, right defensive end position. On the snap, Darren could tell from Nolan's set that the play was going to be a quick pass. He confirmed this notion when he peeked into the backfield and saw Houston Christian's quarterback loading up for a throw to his side.

With no time to rush, Darren did what he was taught: he jumped up into the passing lane and swatted the pass down with his big paws. While Darren was in the air, Nolan lifted him higher, and then from the apex, drove him down into the turf. The big offensive tackle fell on top of him, putting all of his weight into Darren's right shoulder.

Darren first felt a crunch and then an electric burn in the shoulder—a searing awareness, like touching the stove with a wet hand. He ripped off his helmet with his good, left arm and clutched at the fire underneath his right shoulder pad.

Coach Adams looked up at the sky and said, "Uh uh."

The rest of the scrimmage was called off.

6

THE NEXT THING DARREN REMEMBERED WAS waking up in a hospital bed. After orienting himself, he recalled being taken to the hospital. He must've dozed off.

His right shoulder was vaguely sore and from the heavy eyelids and cloudy thoughts, he knew he was on something. With a dip further back into his memory he recalled being administered pain medication. He touched the shoulder and a jolt made its way from the joint down to his wrist. There was no doubt about what happened. His shoulder was torn up.

Once the medication wore off just a little his first thought was, *Where is Marquis?*

He touched his shoulder again as a means of manually taking his thoughts away from his brother and onto the pain. The pain in his shoulder was immediate and pressing, while the pain surrounding his concern for his brother was dull and lurking. The space smelled something like bleach and piss, causing Darren to gag. The door opened and Coach Adams walked in. The coach's eyes were lowered to the floor as he neared.

"What day is it?" Darren asked.

"The next day."

"Huh?"

"The day after the scrimmage.

"My shoulder."

"I shouldn't have put you back in. I knew holding you out was the right thing to do."

"Coach."

"It's pretty bad, Darren."

"How bad?"

"You tore the labrum. Your season is over."

Darren dropped his head. His chin sunk into his chest and a stream of warmth came down his cheeks. He didn't make any noise when he cried. His sobs would be safe with Adams.

Coach Adams wanted to cry himself, but held it together for his favorite player. "It's a hard injury, Darren," he said finally.

Darren lifted his chin and cleared his nose. He wiped away his tears with an awkward shift in the hospital bed, almost tipping the IV drip over. Coach Adams settled the pole that held the solution bag.

"I gotta get out of here."

Coach Adams shook his head.

"No," Coach Adams said. "You need to stay here because—"

Darren was slurring when he said, "No, I gotta get out of the Third Ward, Coach. Not the hospital. The Third Ward. I stay here and I'm dead."

Coach nearly broke down when he heard those words. He feared for the potential destruction of Darren's football career—and maybe his life.

"You'll be okay. The shoulder will heal. You'll be back on track to play in college next year," Coach Adams spoke softly, only half-believing his own words. "The doc is going to do the surgery later today. He wants to repair it as quickly as possible."

"You think I'll play again?"

"It's a hard injury, but yes I do."

"Does my mom know?"

"We just reached her. She's on her way. We couldn't get ahold of her last night."

Darren thought to ask Coach Adams if he had heard anything about Marquis, but couldn't force out the words. He figured if there was bad news, he'd find out soon enough when his mother finally did arrive to the hospital.

"Darren," Adams said.

"Yeah?"

"I'm sorry this happened."

Darren didn't respond. He wasn't ready to accept this as his fate. It still felt unreal, something floating above him, and not staring him in the face. He wasn't really there at the hospital with a ripped-up shoulder. That was someone else lying in that bed. *I'll just close my eyes. Let this stuff that's dripping into my veins take me away.* He closed his eyes.

"Your mom will be in to see you before you go to the operating room," Adams said.

Darren kept his eyes shut. He heard Coach Adams's footsteps and then the door open and close. The tears came once again. *This is gonna break me.*

. . . .

Another wakeup call awaited Darren after surgery. The shoulder was tender, and lucky for him the pain medication was stronger this time. Darren moved his limbs as if his entire body had been dipped in molasses. His eyes moved around the room like a lizard's, and it took a few moments for him to put it together. The sky outside the room was dark. His lips were dry like sun-beaten dirt. He licked some of the chalk away from them.

The IV drip above him worked at a steady rate.

A nurse walked in and asked questions with her eyes. Darren didn't reply. She took that as a cue to bring some water, which she fed him through a straw.

"You're likely nauseous right now because of the medication," she echoed. "Once that goes away, we'll get some food in you."

Darren leaned his head back and blinked gelatinously. The nurse was young and she was *fine*.

"How is your pain?" she asked. "From one to ten?"

Darren held both hands up and opened them.

"Ten?" she said, taken aback. "Really?"

Darren nodded.

"Okay," she said. "I'll prep another ten milligrams of morphine."

Darren blinked again and then closed his eyes. He didn't want any more questions from the fine nurse. She was already onto him. His pain wasn't at a ten. He knew it. She knew it. But he needed that morphine. He needed it to sleep more.

7

DARREN'S MOTHER WAS IN HIS RECOVERY ROOM when he opened his eyes in the morning. Her eyes were wet as she stood over him. She gripped his hand, and by the time he noticed her tears, his eyes jumped open.

"What's the matter?" he asked. "Is it Marquis?"

"Marquis?" she said.

"Is he dead?"

"Now why would Marquis be dead? You having a nightmare?"

"He's not dead?"

"No, he ain't dead."

"Where is he?"

"At his apartment, most likely," she said. "I left him a message that you were here. His phone was off. You know how he is."

Darren thought about his brother being on a burner instead of his normal cell phone, but didn't mention it to his mother.

"Oh," Darren said, the pain popping, as he readjusted himself in a manner that took pressure off his shoulder.

"How is your shoulder?"

"Good up until now," he said, looking up to the IV drip.

"Good?" she said. "Are you sure you didn't hurt your head?"

"Forget it."

"Do you want some food? Something to drink?"

"Nah. I want to get up out of here."

"The doctor is gonna come look at you in a little bit. If it looks good, he'll release you today."

"Is Coach here?"

Darren's mother rolled her eyes. "Nah. He went home early this morning. His sorry ass kept trying to reassure me. Saying he's gonna help you get back to a hundred percent." She made a theatrical gesture with her hand. "I should sue that school for messing up your scholarships."

"You can't sue the school. It's football. Stuff happens on the field."

Darren bolted upright. He forgot about the shoulder, and a shot of pain ran straight to his heart.

"Wait," he said, breathless. "Who said anything about my scholarships?"

"I'm sorry," she said. "I didn't mean anything by it."

She pulled away from the bed.

"Did Coach Adams say anything to you about my scholarships?"

She avoided his eyes.

"Mom? What did Coach say about USC and Boise State?"

"Nothing."

Darren chose to believe her because he had no choice at the moment. It didn't matter. He'd find out the truth from Coach Adams soon enough.

"It ain't the coach's fault I got hurt," Darren said.

"Then why did he apologize to me?"

"That's how he is," he said. "He looks out for us like that. Besides, I trust Coach Adams with my life."

"Hmm."

"If you want to put it on anyone, put it on me. I asked him to put me back in the scrimmage. He wanted to hold me out."

"Well, he's the adult! He's supposed—"

"Call the nurse in here," Darren said, tiring of the pointless back and forth. "I'm in pain."

His mother left the room, and the first emotion that flooded his veins was relief. Relief that his mother had exited his room. He loved her, but she could be a handful. Darren needed peace and quiet at the moment.

Darren's mother reentered with the light-skinned nurse following behind. Both women held looks of disgust on their faces. He knew that his mother was the reason for the nurse's scowl.

"Hi Darren," the nurse said, bracing a smile. "How are you?"

"Hey," he said. "I'm in pain. My shoulder is throbbing."

The nurse touched the shoulder delicately and Darren acted as if she had touched a hot nerve. He didn't know where this was coming from. He hated drugs. He never smoked herb with his teammates that liked to. He never touched the powder that his brother pushed.

"That much pain, huh?" the nurse said.

"Yes."

"Okay, I'll be right back with something for you."

The nurse left the room, walking past Darren's mother without comment. The fog had rolled out of Darren's mind. Suddenly, he realized that the hospital bed he lay in was a throne of power. He was the patient. *He* could say when he was in pain. The nurse. She was there *for* him and no mind-reader.

Maybe she doesn't know I'm full of it.

• •

After the surgeon looked at Darren's shoulder and expressed pleasure in its short-term outlook, he decided that Darren could go home. The nurse stabilized the right arm and called for a wheelchair. Darren struggled with the idea of sitting in a wheelchair. Just two days before, he had been a blue-chip athlete, a force on the field. Now, he had to leave the hospital in a wheelchair?

"I don't need that," Darren said to the nurse, as she looked down at the chair.

"Trust me," she said. "You haven't been up on your feet for a couple of days. With all the meds you've been on, walking is going to be a challenge at first."

"Do you know who I am?"

Darren took a half-step away from the bed and nearly fell down. His legs shook under the weight of his body, and the right shoulder slumped lamely, throwing off his balance. He gripped the handle of the chair. The nurse eased him into it. Embarrassed, Darren looked up at her, and she returned a nurturing smile.

"Damn," he said.

"It's okay," she said. "It happens. And by the way, I do know who you are. Your coach wouldn't stop talking about you."

Darren blushed but the darkness of his skin covered it up.

"Change is hard for me," he said.

"Join the club," the nurse said.

"I never got your name," he said.

"Sadie."

"My name's Darren."

"I know," she said with a warm smile. "I'm gonna pick up your medicine from the pharmacy, and then take you to your mother in the lobby. She's waiting for you there."

Sadie returned with a small white bag. She placed it in Darren's lap.

"Now," she said, "the doctor prescribed some pain medication for you. Oxycontin. Have you taken Oxycontin before?"

He shook his head. "Not unless that was Oxycotton—what you call it? Dripping in my IV."

Sadie smiled. "Oxycontin. No, that was morphine. Something a little stronger for right after surgery."

She bent down to get level with Darren sitting in the chair. She dipped her hand into the bag in his lap and pulled out a small bottle of pills.

"You gotta take it easy with these," she said, looking him straight in the eye. Her eyes looked inside of him. Darren again could've sworn that she knew what he was wrestling with. The back and forth thoughts were tiring, and he couldn't wait to leave this place.

"You only take one pill if you're in extreme pain." she said. "Remember like when you first got here?"

Darren nodded.

"I'm gonna tell your mother the same thing."

"One pill," Darren said. "Extreme pain."

"Okay," she said. "Let's go."

Before embarking for the lobby, Darren reached out and touched Sadie's wrist. She looked down at it and then at Darren.

"Sadie," he said. "Thanks."

"Don't mention it. It's my job, Darren."

8

MARQUIS COULD NOW POKE HIS HEAD OUT FROM his hiding space. He and Mike and the rest of his crew had come out victorious in the battle for the Third Ward. All told, there were ten bodies; five on each side. But the five that Marquis, Mike, and their muscle hit on the other side were substantial players who ranked higher than the sacrificial street-level dealers lost on their side. For Marquis, the killings were an unfortunate, yet necessary, part of his business.

When it was safe, and the concessions from rival gangs had been tallied up, Marquis and Mike strutted out in the open again. Marquis had complete control of the Third Ward again.

Marquis still hadn't turned his primary cell phone back on and had no idea what had befallen his little brother. For now, he was happy that the violence was over though he also knew there would always be more to come in the Third Ward.

Marquis was standing outside a corner market at the intersection of Velasco and Beulah, while Mike was inside getting a couple of sandwiches. The market was situated on valuable turf that Marquis and Mike's crew had just spilled blood for. This corner was a prize—a prime location, with a vast and reputable history of selling product, so much so that the location even attracted users who didn't call the Third Ward home. Marquis gazed out at the corner and experienced nothing. No pang of guilt, nor the rush of victorious excitement. The additional wealth he'd earn—the primary reason for the killings—hadn't even crossed his mind. In truth, he was tired. He was thrilled to be out of the safe house on Alabama street and looked forward to sleeping in his own bed downtown.

The door to the market swung open and Mike walked through it cradling a paper bag.

Marquis dipped his hand into the bag and reached for the tall canister of Arnold Palmer he had ordered. He pulled out a two-liter of lemon-lime soda instead.

"Mike," Marquis said.

Marquis dipped his finger into the bag and peeked inside. There was a cellophane package of Jolly Ranchers at the bottom.

Mike dropped his head before quickly raising it and meeting Marquis's eyes.

"I got it under control, 'Quis."

"You do?"

"Yeah. It's just, you know. Gotta smooth it out."

Marquis had his doubts but did not speak them.

"Wanna eat in the car?"

"Nah," Marquis replied. "Let's walk."

So they walked down the block away from the market. The streets and corners were still empty, save for a few ambitious dealers who were eager to open shop again. Marquis and Mike walked free and without care. They ate their cold-cut subs and sipped their Arnold Palmers. They stopped at certain points as tacit recollections of past beefs. They lingered in front of a church where a two-year old was shot and killed three summers past. Finally, Marquis balled up his sub wrapper and threw it in a trashcan in front of the church.

They walked again and Marquis reached into his jeans to retrieve his cell. He powered it on and waited for its LED screen to light up. He knew there'd be a load of messages, but when he focused on the numerous calls from his mother, his brow furrowed.

"We gotta cut this short," Marquis said.

"What's up?" Mike replied.

"I'll tell you in the car," Marquis said.

. . . .

Darren's mother drove him home from the hospital,

and on the way, Darren looked out of the window. People were back out working the corners, letting him know that whatever beef there was, it had been sorted out. And from the familiarity of the faces working the corners, it was clear that Marquis had won something.

"Where's my brother?" Darren asked his mother, as they pulled up to the front of the house.

"I don't know," she said. "Hasn't called me back yet. I'm gonna let him have it when I see him 'round here."

"You call him on his cell?"

"Yeah, at least ten times."

"He's been on a burner, last week or so."

Darren's mother glanced over at him as she turned off the ignition and pulled out the key.

"Anyways," she said. "You home. Let's get you inside and on the couch."

They went inside and Darren plopped down on the couch in the living room. His mother went straight to the kitchen, opened the fridge, and pulled the ring off a can. Darren could hear her take a long pull. She exhaled deeply and placed the can on the counter with a tinny echo.

"You hungry?" she asked. "Need anything?"

"Just water."

Darren turned on the TV and flipped around. He stopped first at ESPN, but the thought of sports depressed him. He settled on one of those drug king-pin shows. Darren's mother walked over with a bottle of water in one hand and her can in the other. She set the water on the coffee table in front of him.

"I'm gonna be upstairs. Holler if you need me."

"Okay," he said.

As soon as she went upstairs, Darren conducted a pain test on the shoulder. It was still raw to be sure, but the level of pain had definitely gone down. He rotated the shoulder slowly and got the jolt he was looking for. The area around the incision burned, and Darren gritted his teeth. He went for the white bag and lifted the pill bottle out of it. He popped the top and shook out two of the fat white pills. He drank half the water from the bottle and leaned back on the couch.

The show was just starting. The thirty-minute program promised to follow the life of a well-known dealer from Washington, D.C. Darren's brother, Marquis, loved these shows. Darren asked Marquis one time if he wanted to have a show like this made about him. Marquis chuckled and said he did, but not yet.

Darren's head was fuzzy when the show touched on the dealer's rise to stardom on the corners, and within row houses of our nation's capitol. A ludicrous smile curled onto Darren's face and he forgot all his troubles. Football was a foreign thought to him now. The torn shoulder was distant. His mother, his brother? They didn't exist in this space. A dab of drool dripped down the left side of Darren's mouth. He wiped at it without accuracy.

When the first commercial came, Darren's eyelids became heavy. *Damn, where has this been my whole life?* He was feeling good, light as a feather. He fought off the sleep and made it to the next segment. The D.C. kingpin was a bad dude, known to have over two hundred bodies on him. Darren closed his eyes and fell into a warm, wet sleep. He could hear the TV a while with his eyes closed, but eventually, Darren had more important business to get to in his dreams.

These weren't the type of dreams that are normally labeled as good—Darren didn't lead Sunnyside to a win in State or make it to the NFL. He dreamed about being somewhere else. Somewhere he couldn't name or identify. Some place safe. A gunshot blared out of the TV and caused Darren to jump awake. He looked around and the living room. *Okay, where am I? Is this real?*

He looked around the room some more. There was the pill bottle. A half-empty bottle of water. The TV was on. The show was the same, but a different kingpin was the focus now. *This* episode was about the badass player from Mexico. The dude who everyone feared and respected. Marquis thought the *amigo* was a real boss-player, *El-something. What was that dude's name again?* Darren couldn't remember. He popped two more fat white pills, leaned back on the couch, and got an education.

. . . .

"Darren," a voice whispered. "Yo, Darren."

Darren eyes flickered open and shut. He blinked a few times. The TV was off.

"How are you?" the voice asked, a little louder. "I heard you messed up your shoulder."

With a few more blinks, the focus returned. Darren saw Marquis standing before him.

"Marquis."

"Yeah."

"You're alive."

"Of course I'm alive."

"I thought you were," Darren said, before licking his lips. "I thought you were . . . can you pass me that water?"

Marquis handed the bottle of water to Darren.

He opened the cap and drank from it, draining the rest. Marquis saw the bottle of pills on the table in front of Darren. He picked it up and read the label.

"What are these?" Marquis asked.

Darren lowered his eyes. "For my shoulder."

"Yeah?"

"I'm supposed to take them when I'm in pain."

"Well, are you in pain?"

"Usually, yeah. But at the moment, no."

Marquis eyed his little brother. He knew drugs and drug users.

"Be careful with these Oxys. Folks get hooked on 'em easy. It's like heroin. It *is* heroin. You ain't careful and you turn into one of them fiends out there."

Marquis jabbed a thumb behind him, that presumably meant the Third Ward.

"They're just for the pain," Darren repeated, a hint of defensiveness in his tone. "I'm fresh out of surgery."

"I heard. So tell me what happened?"

Marquis sat down on the couch next to Darren.

"I jumped up to bat down a pass. Their big-ass tackle caught me in the air and came down right on my shoulder."

"Damn. Did it hurt?"

"Worst pain ever."

"You out for the season?"

"That's what Coach said."

Marquis sighed. "You still have your offers, right?"

"I haven't heard anything about them," Darren said. "I don't see why the schools would pull them."

"They're dirty, that's why," he said. "They don't care about you. Ask Coach Adams about your offers when you see him."

"A'ight."

"Better yet, call him tomorrow and ask about your offers."

Darren nodded.

"When are you going back to school?"

"What day is it?"

"Monday. Damn nigga, did you hit your head too?"

"I'm not gonna go this week," Darren said, rubbing at his shoulder. "I can't focus in class with this. Maybe I'll go back at the beginning of next week."

Marquis nodded and said, "A'ight. You hungry?"

"Nah. My appetite is gone."

Marquis stood up. "Hit me on my regular number if you need me. I gotta bounce right now. Take care of a few things."

Darren nodded, while looking at the floor.

"Darren?" Marquis asked.

Darren raised his eyes and looked up at his older brother.

"You got a problem with these pills?"

"Me? Nah, I'm not a fiend."

"I didn't say you were a fiend. I'm just saying that sometimes these pills can cause problems."

"I don't have a problem. I just took one since I've been out of surgery."

"Just one?"

"I just took one."

A burdensome silence fell between the two brothers. Both had questions for the other, but neither had the heart to ask them. Marquis *knew* something was up with Darren and the Oxys—Darren looked dusty, a Third Ward word for the fiends with foggy minds and runny noses. Marquis looked into his brother's eyes and searched for the clue that any junkie would drop. The clue was always in the eyes. Marquis had learned the lesson early in life, while out on the corners. Darren's eyes were glazed, a far cry from the focused, laser beams he exhibited on the field.

Darren had intuitive knowledge too, that his brother had just finished spilling blood out in the Third Ward.

"Yeah well, call me if you need anything," Marquis said. "This ain't a big deal. You heal up and go back to school. Life goes on. I'll come see you tomorrow. Bring you some food."

"A'ight," Darren said.

Marquis walked to the front door.

"Oh. How is Mom?" Darren asked. "I fell asleep right after we got home from the hospital. She went upstairs before."

"Mom's asleep. She's fine."

The brothers shared a knowing glance in silence, but once again neither had the fortitude to say what needed to said.

"Take care out there, 'Quis."

Marquis smiled at the fact that his younger brother was worried about him out in the Third Ward. He owned the Third Ward.

"*You*, take care," Marquis said.

Darren nodded. Marquis left the house and approached his Expedition. He sat in his truck outside of his mother's house for awhile before leaving. Something was going on with Darren and those pills. It was against his better judgment to leave the Oxys there with Darren. But with all his rough edges, Marquis had soft spots as well. His mother was a soft spot, even with all her drinking and whatnot.

Darren was the biggest soft spot of all. He did not want his little brother experiencing any pain.

9

POST-SURGERY, DARREN SET UP CAMP IN THE LIVING room and woke up abnormally early, on the couch, exactly two weeks after he had been home from the hospital. He had not gone back to school yet. He had taken exactly two Oxys per day—one in the morning and one before bed—during the past week. Nothing too risky, it seemed.

He hadn't behaved like an abuser that first week; he had *controlled* how many pills he took and made sure not to go overboard. Plus, *this* was the day he would kick them for good—the use of painkillers for one week after surgery was normal, certainly nothing to set off any alarms. And finally, his supply was running low, only two pills left.

There was one problem. His shoulder actually hurt that morning. The pain was at a ten. He stood up from the couch, thinking that with blood flow, the shoulder would loosen up. Wrong. He could barely stand because of the pain. *What if I just take the last two now to get rid of the pain?*

He checked the clock on the DVD player and it read six thirty. His mother was not awake yet. The house was still. *Maybe I need to get some food up in me. Yeah. That's it. After I eat, the pain will go away.*

Darren got up off the couch and withstood the shooting pains in his right arm. The arm sagged as he walked into the kitchen. He opened the fridge with his left hand. His mother rarely went shopping, and with Marquis being so busy with his reorganization of the Third Ward's corners, the fridge was cavernous in its emptiness.

Damn.

Darren slammed the door shut and the aftershock

sent a burn from shoulder to fingertips. *Just two pills to get me through the morning.* He walked over to the coffee table and took the pill bottle into his hands. He shook the last two out and dry swallowed them. He reached down for the remote control and powered on the TV. The pills took hold pretty quickly. He collapsed onto the couch and started looking for something to watch. Fifteen minutes later, he was knocked out. As far away from southeast Houston as one person could be without actually leaving.

．．．．．．．．．．．．．．．．．．．．．．．．．．．

Marquis woke up late that next morning. There was a lot of work to be done now that he controlled things outright. He had to whip a couple of new crews into shape for starters, but could easily put Mike on that. He also needed to name a new lieutenant with Shorty Boy pushing up daisies.

He grabbed the carton of orange juice out of the otherwise empty fridge in his downtown Houston condo. He took deep, thoughtful sips as he stared out of a large bay window. A long way from the Third Ward, he thought.

He went into his bedroom to get dressed because Mike would be there any minute for a meeting. One of his lady friends was still in bed when he walked in. He rotated girlfriends because he was young and didn't want to spend the cash it took to keep one girl happy. He ruffled the covers and she shifted, exposing her naked rear end.

"You got to get up," he said.

"No breakfast?" she replied.

"Here's twenty, you can hit up Denny's. I'm sorry baby. Business."

He tossed the bill on the bed cover.

She turned her head to look at him. He was sliding on some jeans when he caught her glance.

"Yeah. Yeah. I know," she said.

She rose up out of bed and slid on her clothes, making her way to the master bathroom. After a few minutes, she came out, looking good as new and picked up the twenty dollars before leaving without saying goodbye.

Mike knocked on the door ten minutes later. Marquis let him in, and they walked to that prime spot in front of the bay window.

"I can't get over this view," Mike gushed.

"Yeah," Marquis said, not able to hide his contentment over his spot.

Mike rubbed his hands together like always.

"You want something?" Marquis asked, holding the fridge door open. "There ain't much, but . . . "

"Nah, I'm cool."

Marquis closed the fridge and inspected his partner; Mike's eyes looked clear and unburdened.

"How you doing with the lean?'" Marquis asked. "You been sippin'?"

Mike shook his head. "Nah, boss. I'm doing good. Better."

"Let's get to it, then."

They walked over to the dining room table and sat.

"You get rid of the guns?"

"Yeah," Mike said.

"All of them?"

"In the drain."

"Good. I need you to go over to the 'hood after this," Marquis said. "We own a couple new crews as you know. I want you to go over and let them niggas know what's what."

"Got it," Mike said. "Anything else?"

"With Shorty-Boy out, we got an open crew-chief spot. Any thoughts about who that should go to?"

"You want my opinion?"

"Yeah. You stepped up on this last turn. I'll never forget that," Marquis said, tapping his heart with his right hand, "I'm gonna be askin' your opinion on things now."

Mike's face swelled with pride.

"This is the first thing," Marquis added.

"Well, I know Dougie would die for crew chief," Mike suggested. "He's been running Drew Street, and he dropped one on the other side during this little scuffle."

"Dougie?" Marquis said, screwing his face at the thought. "He worries me with his wildness. A nigga like that wanna get caught."

"I'll talk to him."

"Cool."

"We good?"

Marquis nodded and stood up from the table. Mike did the same. The two friends shook hands and half-hugged.

"I got a meeting today," Marquis said. "Hit me on the cell if you need any guidance."

"Got it."

"Oh," Marquis said before walking into the kitchen. He opened a drawer and pulled out a letter-sized manilla envelope. He handed the envelope to Mike. "This is for you."

Mike opened it and found ten thousand dollars, in banded, cleanly crisp bills.

"For your pain," Marquis said.

10

DARREN WOBBLED UPSTAIRS TO HIS ROOM TO GRAB some cash stashed in a shoebox, given to him by Marquis. His pain was gone, replaced by something much worse. The bottle was empty.

He used the handrail to get back downstairs. The time was twelve noon. Darren needed two things: food and pills. This stint, sedentary sadness combined with poor eating—sometimes not eating at all—left his stomach a queasy, fist of knots. He counted out the money that Marquis had given him. Three hundred dollars. *Plenty.*

He wiggled himself into a hoodie, pulled the hood over his head and left through the front door.

Darren would need to play this cool. Everyone knew him in the Third Ward. Especially the dealers. Many, if not all, worked for Marquis.

He ducked into the market on Velasco and Beulah to think over his plan while waiting for a turkey breast sub on wheat. When he received his order, he didn't come close to finishing the food—a rare thing before the shoulder injury. His stomach growled and moaned at Darren's inconsistent approach toward filling it. The shoulder started aching again, and a sheet of sweat formed on his brow. He didn't take his hood down because he would be exposed without it. Instead of thinking it over, he had settled. He *had* to get something for the pain.

Darren staggered out of the carryout and headed toward the hot corners he knew. He had never done anything like this before. *Do these jokers out here even have Oxys?* He didn't have the courage to walk up to any of the dealers he knew by name, so he walked a little further away to less familiar grounds.

When he reached the high-rise terrace apartments, he stopped. He remembered overhearing Marquis; that the towers were prime location for slanging. There were a couple of boys standing near the entrance to south tower's lobby. They surveyed Darren. Darren didn't know either of them by sight. He approached with caution and noticed that there were two other groups of boys working lookout on either side of the towers. The two boys in front eyed him as he neared.

"What'chu want?" one the boys asked.

"I, uh," Darren said, trying to sink his eyes further beneath the hood. "I'm looking for Oxys."

The two boys looked at each other and laughed.

"Oxys?" the other one said. "What you think this is, a pharmacy?"

They laughed some more.

"Boy, this is dope, coke and if you come on a good day, I can *maybe* get you some ice," the first one said.

"Ice goes fast," the other one chimed in.

"Oh, uh, my bad," Darren said.

"But you know what?" the first one said with fire in his entrepreneurial eyes. "Dope is just like Oxy. It's the same thing"

"Yeah, they come from the same family," the second one said with a snap.

"Nah. It's okay," Darren said, taking a step back.

"Don't leave so quickly," the first one said. "We can get you what you need."

"I said, I'm good," Darren said.

The first one narrowed his eyes. A note of recognition came onto his face.

"You don't need to be a little punk about it!" the second one spewed, taking a step toward Darren.

The first one put out his arm and blocked his associate from getting any closer.

"It's cool," the first one said. "Let him roll out."

Darren turned around and left.

The second boy stared at Darren's back with disdain, until he turned a corner and went out of sight.

"Do you know who that was?" the first boy asked.

"That big dude?" the second boy replied. "Nah, can't say I do."

"That's the big man's little brother."

"Marquis's little brother?" the second replied with mouth agape. "Darren?"

The first boy nodded.

"I thought he plays football at Sunnyside. He's supposed to be big time."

"He does play," the first one said. "And he is big time. I saw him play last season."

"He hooked on Oxys?"

"I guess. I wonder if Marquis knows."

"You don't think Darren is gonna tell 'Quis that I stepped to him, do you?" the second boy asked with a gulp.

"Nah. You're good."

A black Expedition pulled up in front of the towers. Marquis had loaned the Expedition to Mike as a way to assist him in his meetings with the displaced Third Ward crews. The austere ride personified respect and strength and, if you were on Marquis's bad side, fear. Mike got out of the driver's side and a large man wearing a sleeveless shirt got out of the passenger's side. They approached. Mike rubbed his hands together.

"Fellas," Mike said.

The two boys who worked in front of the towers were a part of the losing side in the battle against Marquis and his crew. The pawns were now in the process of being placed under the umbrella of Marquis's operation as the reorganization commenced. Mike's arrival to the towers that morning represented the beginning of a new partnership.

"You're doing the right thing by makin' this easy," Mike said. "You and your people are gonna make money with us."

The two boys looked at each other and then to Mike.

"Right. Yeah," the first one said. "Before we talk business. Marquis has a younger brother, right? Plays football?"

"Yeah, why?"

The two boys looked at each other again.

"Boy got a problem," the first one said.

. . . .

Sadie stood at the nurses' station. She dropped a patient's folder into the *out* bin and then went over to check on another patient. A page came over the intercom for her. She was wanted in the waiting room. It wasn't a nine-one-one page, but she hustled over nonetheless. Sadie was shocked to see Darren standing before her.

"Were you the one who paged me?" she asked.

"Yeah," he said. "I didn't put you out, did I?"

"No, it's okay," she said. "What's up?"

"Well my shoulder has been killing me, and I was wondering if I could get some more of those pills."

"You left here with a month's supply, Darren. That was two weeks ago."

"I know," he said. "It's just that . . . "

"I can't do it. And also, the fact that you are here, seeking drugs—I have to report it."

"Report it?" Darren's eyes lit up. "Report what?"

"This," she said. "Either you're abusing the pills or selling them."

"Selling them? No you got the wrong idea, Sadie. You got the wrong brother."

"You need to leave now."

Sadie turned her back to Darren and started to leave.

"Wait," he said. "I'm in pain."

She turned to him and approached slowly. Sadie came close enough to where she didn't need to speak loudly. She spoke slowly because she wanted him to hear her, and she wanted him to get it.

"You're big," she said. "A big football player. But you're not that big. We've had players in here who play for the Texans that are twice as big as you, and they didn't need half the dosage you left here with."

Darren tried to pull away but Sadie grabbed his left arm.

"You need to get out of here right now. And you need to stop looking for pills."

Darren lowered his eyes to floor.

"Got it?"

He raised his eyes and met hers.

"Yeah, I got it," he said.

She let go of his arm and walked back into the ER. Darren turned and walked out of the hospital.

When Sadie reached the nurses' station, she sat down to think for a moment. It was the first time during that day's eight hour shift that she had had a moment off her feet. She exhaled. It felt good. She stood up and went inside an open office adjacent to the nurses' station. The office held the records of patients who had come through the ER. Darren's file would be in the cabinet marked discharged. She found his file within the batch and opened it. She saw that Darren attended Sunnyside High School and picked up the phone.

11

MARQUIS SAT IN THE TWENTIETH FLOOR OFFICE of a downtown Houston insurance firm. The man whose office it was, was white, thin, in his forties, and wore a three-piece suit.

"Thanks for coming in, Mr. Taylor," he said.

Marquis's phone buzzed in his pocket. He reached for it and read the display. It was Mike. Marquis turned down the call.

"Do you need to take that?" the man asked.

"Uh-uh," Marquis said. "It's not important."

"Well what is it that I can do for you?"

"I want to take out an insurance policy."

"For what?"

"My little brother. Darren," Marquis said. "He plays ball over at Sunnyside High. Third Ward. He has a couple D-I offers. Could probably go pro if it broke right for him. See the thing is, he just tore up his shoulder a week ago in a scrimmage and now he's out for his senior season. We're not sure if the two colleges are gonna pull their scholarship offers. Darren's coach is waiting to hear back. So I'm trying to protect my little brother against that."

"You're saying he's an 'exceptional student-athlete?'"

"Damn right."

"I see. Would you be willing to disclose the names of the two universities?"

Marquis shrugged.

"USC and Boise State."

"Good schools."

"My little brother is dope."

The man wrote the names of the two schools down on a notepad.

"So how do we do this?" Marquis asked.

"In an effort to gauge Darren's financial worth, we must first put the pieces together to deem your brother a 'potential professional.'"

"To see if Darren is an 'exceptional student athlete?'"

"Yes."

"And how do you put those pieces together?"

"I'd have to have my independent analyst look at Darren's high school career, make calls to the interested schools, and discuss Darren with an NFL scout that he trusts. And then we'd go from there."

"Yeah?" Marquis said as he scratched at the hair on his chin.

"That work is gonna cost—and you'd have to foot the bill—but it's the only way to come up with a true figure that reflects your brother's value."

"Okay. I'm down with paying for that."

"And this work would be independent of you potentially taking out a policy with us. I just want that to be clear."

"It's clear."

"Then there's also the question of collateral."

"You mean how will I pay for the policy?"

The man smiled in that sheepish way that all intermediaries in suits smile.

"Cash work?" Marquis said.

"Cash works fine."

Marquis stood up. "That's a bet then. Call me when your man gives you his report on Darren."

The man in the suit stood up from behind his desk. He extended his hand out to Marquis. "I'll get my analyst started. Projecting Darren's future all the way to the NFL will be a bit tricky, but let's first see what all the football people have to say. No matter what, if Darren never plays another down again or let's say he makes it to college and hurts the same shoulder again, ending his career. He'll be able to collect on the policy that we agree on."

Marquis shook the man's hand and left the office. Before stepping into a down elevator, Marquis dialed Mike. It rang three times before Mike answered.

"Yo, you call me?" Marquis said into the receiver.

"Yeah, 'Quis, what's up?"

"You called me."

"Right. I don't mean to bother. I know you had a meeting. But there's something that needs your attention."

"Spit it, nigga."

The elevator doors clapped and Marquis went down.

* *

Darren didn't know where to go next. All he knew was that he felt pain—real pain. The shoulder burned with every step and when the sizzling sensation subsided, that's when the constant throbbing returned. A persistent ache that threatened to drive Darren mad. He thought about going back to a corner and copping some dope, but decided against it. He had forgotten about everything else in his life—football, his family. None of it mattered.

His phone rang and he took it out of a front jean pocket. It was Marquis. He didn't accept the call. *Should I call Coach Adams? Maybe he could help me out of this?*

He scrolled through his contacts and found Coach Adams's number. He almost pressed the *call* button but didn't. He turned off his phone and continued walking, crossed back into the Third Ward, and passed a few "live" corners without stopping.

Darren reached his house. He had no pills and even worse, Marquis's Expedition was parked out front, marking a clear change in Darren's thinking. He could not face Marquis in the condition he was in. He walked past his house and kept walking for a while, until he reached a block—the intersection of Live Oak and Isabella—which he did not know, but more importantly, where he was not known.

I can definitely cop here.

In front of a squat, one-story ranch home, stood two boys—around Darren's age—dressed in black. They had the look of dealers, and Darren managed to lock eyes with the taller of the two, even though his face was buried inside his hood. The tall boy in black held a bland countenance without a glint of recognition across the eyes.

"What's up?" Darren asked on the approach.

"Nothing," the tall one said.

"Yo, you got any Oxys?"

"No pills," the tall one said. "Dope or coke."

This was the place Darren thought he'd never be. Making a decision that he never thought he'd face. Up to that point, he had thought his biggest decision would be about college.

"Let me get three *tens* of dope."

Darren figured he'd just snort the heroine, because of his fear of needles.

"Buy an extra two, I'll throw in one more for free."

"Just the three, is all," Darren said. His eyes sunk deeper into his hood.

"That'll be thirty."

Darren reached in his pocket and pulled out his

money. He forgot one of the golden rules his brother had taught him early on.

"Oh!" the tall one said.

Darren never realized that he had been cracked on the jaw by a chrome-plated, semi-automatic pistol because he was knocked out on impact. The blow was flush on the chin and it put Darren down. The two boys in black rifled through his pockets—finding his cell phone and nothing else of value—before simply settling on the cash he had on him.

"Why you do it?" the short one asked. "It's not even that much bread."

"You know the rule," the tall one replied. "'Never flash your cash.' I had to school him. Here, help me move him down the block, away from the shop. He's big."

They took hold of Darren, one at each end, and when it became clear that they weren't going to be able to move him far, they put him back down.

"See? You stupid," the short one blurted. "You

should've thought about it first before you hit him for two hundred and change. Now what are we gonna do?"

"Shut up, nigga."

The tall one looked down and focused on Darren's face. He bent over and peeled the hood back.

"Damn."

"What is it?" the short one said, as he lit up a Black and Mild.

"Do you know who this is?"

The short one got a better look at Darren's face, now that there was no hood obscuring it.

The two partners exchanged looks that conveyed first, shock, then, remorse.

"What are we gonna do?" the short one asked. "That's the big man's little brother."

"What is he doing out here?"

The tall one stepped away from Darren and put his face in his hands. He thought about how this could get settled without him and his partner being killed.

"Let me see his phone," the tall one said.

The short one tossed Darren's cell phone over. The tall one scrolled through Darren's contact list and found the entry for 'Quis. He pressed the *call* button and waited for a ring.

Marquis was sitting on the couch in his mother's living room when his cell phone rang. The screen read "D" and he accepted the call.

"Where are you, D? I'm waiting at the house for you."

"This ain't D," the voice on the other end said.

Marquis leaned forward. "Who is this?"

"I found D lying here at the corner of Live Oak and Isabella. Some niggas—three of them, I think—rolled him for his cash. One of them, lost his composure and pistol-whipped D. He's knocked out on the sidewalk."

Marquis was silent, frozen. The words coming from the other end of the line seemed unreal and hadn't registered.

"Hello?" the voice on the other end asked.

Marquis snapped back to life before hanging up his phone. He streaked out of the front door and into his truck.

The tall one hung up Darren's phone and placed it on his chest.

"We should keep his money. Make sure it looks like a robbery."

"Good idea."

"Let's bounce."

The boys in black bolted away from Darren's body, splayed out along the sidewalk.

· ·

Darren woke up in a hospital bed. There was a swath of soreness somewhere on his face. As he put a hand to his chin, there was the bandage between thumb and skin. As he surveyed the room with caution, he noticed that Marquis was there, sitting in a chair by his bed. He looked like he had been crying, but that couldn't have been right.

"What's going on?" Darren asked. His throat was dry and his shoulder was sore all over again, sensitive to the slightest movements.

Marquis cleared his throat. "You're back up in the hospital." His eyes didn't move when he spoke, instead, focusing on the rail of the hospital bed. They were sad and tired.

"What time is it?"

"Just past midnight."

"My head," Darren said. "I don't know what happened."

"Life is like that," Marquis said, blinking lazily. "You get into something and you don't even realize that you're in it."

Sadie walked into the room, carrying a cup of water and small paper cup with two pills in it. Though a staunch proponent of professionalism, she could not resist a glance into Darren's eyes when she got close.

"What are these?" Darren demanded, hoping a change of subject would ease the spotlight over top of him.

"*Vitamins*," she said. "You were dehydrated. You haven't been eating."

Darren looked behind him and saw the IV dripping.

"It's just a sugar drip to give you energy," she said. "You'll get no more drugs in here."

Sadie walked out of the room.

Marquis moved his chair closer to Darren.

"I should've taken those pills away from you the first night you got out of the hospital for your shoulder."

A passing thought of Mike and his trouble with lean struck Marquis, and he became transfixed on the railing again.

"You okay, 'Quis?"

Marquis looked into his brother's eyes and at first it seemed like the two had never met. "Huh? Yeah. I'm good."

Darren dry gulped because he couldn't think of anything to say.

"I *should've* snatched 'em off that goddamn coffee

table," Marquis said before a pregnant pause, "but I didn't."

Marquis's eyes went distant yet again. He had always separated his job from his family. They never crossed paths because he always kept them apart. But now, things were tangled. The problem wasn't only that Darren was hooked. There were other things to consider. The streets don't reward the weak. Marquis would have to retaliate against those who beat and robbed his little brother. If he wanted to keep his spot at the top of the Third Ward, he'd have to have those boys killed.

His eyes finally moved to Darren and the image of his little brother with two of his bottom teeth knocked clean out, made Marquis think that *maybe* he didn't want the top spot any longer. That *maybe* the crown didn't mean what it used to mean to him—just one day before. The potential for change, the violent swiftness of it, the thought of even beginning to change, shook him.

"But you ain't never gonna have another pill on

my watch," Marquis mustered jaggedly, while looking at the floor.

There was a savage rush of silence in the room. Neither brother drew a breath.

"You okay?" Darren asked. "You look white. I mean, your skin."

"That nurse, Sadie, she's a good woman," Marquis said. His breath was hurried and flowing out of him now. "She called Sunnyside. She talked to Coach Adams. You're gonna have to deal with the pain in your shoulder *and* your jaw. Not so much as an aspirin is going into your body."

The warm pool in Darren's eyes stung him. He was scared for the first time in his life. Having Marquis as an older brother usually shielded him from that emotion.

"And as soon as you get up out of here, your ass is going back to school. You can go to class with a sore shoulder. You can learn with a stitched-up lip."

Marquis took a deep breath, stood up, and walked to the window, darkened by the night sky.

"I'm gonna be around more," Marquis said, with his back to Darren.

He turned around to face his little brother.

Darren wiped his face, leaned his head back and closed his eyes.

"Let me make something clear to you, Darren. The way I live ain't never gonna be the way you live. And I'm not playing. You're going back to class. You're gonna heal and get back on the field. Then you're going to college. You ain't living my life."

12

DARREN STAYED AT THE HOSPITAL FOR ANOTHER two days—mainly due to the fact that an orthodontist had to come in to fit Darren for replacement crowns on his bottom row. Marquis was by his little brother's side the whole time. Sadie reworked her schedule to stay on as Darren's nurse for the duration of his stay. Marquis appreciated that. He asked Sadie if she would go out with him—explaining that finding a good woman was the first step in getting this new start that was brewing inside of him. Sadie told Marquis that she'd think about it, but to not get his hopes up.

The evening before the hospital released Darren, another doctor fit the surgically repaired shoulder into a sling and stitched up the gash right under his lip. The swelling in his jaw had gone down considerably, and after being cleaned up, the gash looked like it could've been caused by a punch rather than a gun. The sling helped right away too; the shoulder moved around less and caused less irritation for Darren.

The next morning, Marquis drove Darren home to get changed for school. There weren't any words exchanged on the car ride home. Darren looked out the window like always. Marquis pulled up to the house and parked the car. Darren unbuckled his seatbelt with his off-hand and looked at Marquis.

"You're not coming in?"

"Nah," Marquis said, checking his watch. "Hurry up, you're gonna be late."

"What about Mom?"

"What about her? She's probably not up."

Darren opened the door.

"You remember how to put the sling back on, right?" Marquis said.

Darren nodded and walked into the house. He went up into his room and changed clothes. He grabbed his backpack. In the living room, he checked the floor around the couch to see if he dropped any pills from the original bottle.

He stood up and went out through the front door. In the Expedition, Marquis's phone rang. It was the man from the insurance office.

"Hello?"

"Yes, Mr. Taylor."

"Oh yeah, what's up?"

"Just wanted to update you as to the initial findings of my associate."

"Yeah, damn. I totally forgot about that. Something went down and I got tied up," Marquis said.

"I understand."

"I'll be in touch today or the next day."

"Sounds good, Mr. Taylor."

Marquis hung up his phone.

"Who was that?" Darren asked.

"Nobody. Did you get all of your books?"

"Yeah."

Marquis started the truck and pulled out of the driveway. Once again, the ride was quiet. Marquis's head was swimming. Not only was he worried about his little brother's future, he was now worried about his own. *Maybe* it was all wrong and had been wrong from the start?

Darren's thoughts were simpler. He wondered how he was going to get through the day without an Oxy.

The Expedition pulled up in front of Sunnyside High. Darren unbuckled and opened the door with his off arm—the injured right arm slung close to his chest. Marquis put a hand on Darren's left forearm.

"I'll be here," Marquis said. "Call me if you need anything."

"A'ight."

Darren got out of the truck and loped up the walk and into school. Marquis watched him until he entered through the front doors and then pulled his truck into the faculty lot in back of school. He made sure to park in a spot that had a view of the various back exits. The front exit would be covered by school security. If Darren tried to bolt the back way, Marquis would know it.

His phone rang again as he turned off the truck's ignition. The display read *Mike.*

"Mike."

"'Quis," Mike said.

"What's up?"

"I wanted to check in with you."

Marquis thought for a moment. "I want you to run things the next couple of days," Marquis said. "I gotta stay with Darren. There's no other way to make sure he's straight."

There was a pause on the line, the only sound that could be heard was Mike's heavy breathing.

"You there?" Marquis asked.

"Yeah," Mike said.

"You can handle this, right?"

"No doubt."

"Call me if there's drama."

"That's a bet."

"Oh and don't worry about hitting those boys back—the ones that rolled D. Call off the search."

Another heavy silence hung on the line.

"You sure? These little niggas put hands on Darren."

"Call it off."

Marquis hung up and spun the dial of his truck's radio into the *on* position.

* *

Darren was a foreigner in the halls that he once owned. The discerning eyes of classmates were on him. The nods of reverence were replaced with something icky and scandalous. He was convinced that everyone in school thought he was a dope fiend.

He glued his eyes to the floor as he made his way to Coach Adams's office. He had a meeting with him before first period. The urge to break out and find pills was deep. It weighed him down. His stomach was queasy and his head was light. He sweat through his clothes as he made the long walk to the locker room. *How am I going to make it through this day?*

Darren walked up to the door and knocked softly. He actually thought about leaving—blowing off the meeting, setting fire to his future. The locker room had an exit that only the athletes knew about. On second thought, he remembered that Marquis was on him, and most likely waiting outside in the Expedition.

He knocked a little louder and it roused Coach Adams.

"Come in!"

Darren walked into the office and stood in front of the desk. Coach Adams held a somber look on his face.

"Hello Darren."

"Hey Coach."

Darren couldn't raise his eyes. He was sad for letting Coach Adams down. After all, he was the first person to give Darren responsibility—over the defense, over the team. *And this is how I repaid that trust?* Darren just wanted to feel like himself again, but he didn't know how.

"Have a seat, son."

Darren sat and put his backpack on the floor. He rearranged his sling so the shoulder wouldn't ache.

"How is your shoulder?"

"Okay," Darren said.

"And your chin?"

Darren shrugged.

"A nurse called me from the hospital," Adams said. "Your brother too."

Darren lowered his eyes again.

"They both said you had some trouble after surgery."

Darren lifted his head. His eyes watered, but didn't stream. "I'm sorry, Coach."

Coach Adams got up and walked around his desk.

"You don't have anything to be sorry about," he said.

"I let you down."

"No. That's not true. You didn't let me down. This isn't an ending for you, son."

Coach Adams hugged Darren, careful not to bang into the shoulder, and Darren hugged him back.

"There's something I need to tell you, Darren."

Darren looked up.

"USC pulled its offer."

The first wave that hit Darren was sickness. He stared straight ahead as his empty stomach churned in on itself.

Coach Adams continued, "That's their right. They're worried about your shoulder. They don't think you'll ever be the same. I say forget about them."

Darren's eyes went blank. Coach's words were just that, words. They had no meaning or bearing. Darren was floating.

"The good news is, Boise State hasn't given up on you. The school is willing to honor its offer if it sees that you take rehab seriously. And let me tell you, this is good news. Not that you need any extra incentive to get yourself back into playing condition. But now, just in case you need a little push, it's there."

"I don't know if I can do it, Coach," Darren said, coming out with it. USC had placed him in the grave, and the trouble with the pills was the proverbial dirt being shoveled on top of his casket. "I've never been injured before. And I'm dealing with this other thing too. I don't know."

Coach Adams took a deep breath. He patted Darren's healthy shoulder.

"I'm going to see you through this. Getting your shoulder healthy. The pills. All of it. I'll never turn my back on you. I'm here for you. You'll get your college scholarship. I'm gonna see to it."

Darren didn't respond.

The bell rang for first period.

"Go on to class," he said. "The trainer is gonna examine your shoulder after school, and then you'll be out there at practice with the team. I don't want you thinking that you're not a part of this. You're a big part of this."

Darren nodded at Coach Adams, but his mind had moved back to those fat white pills. He stood up and realized that his t-shirt was stuck to his back because of how much he was sweating.

He walked out of Coach Adams's office and into the locker room. He remembered that he had a clean t-shirt in his locker. He changed into it and sat down in front of his locker. This was his spot, where he could block out the noise and find peace. He took a deep breath, and the desperation and desolation from Coach Adams's office seemed to wear off. The thought of yo-yoing back and forth from under control to disarray was scarier than the actual addiction itself. He looked up and one of the secret locker room exits was right there, staring right at him.

13

DARREN COULDN'T HEAR WHAT HIS FIRST PERIOD teacher was saying. This was different than when Darren had *chosen* not to pay attention in class. That had been a free and democratic choice. Now there was simply too much noise in his head.

Maybe I could sneak into the nurse's office? Wait, a school nurse won't have Oxys. She probably only has Tylenol.

A few of his teammates in first period offered words of consolation about the shoulder. No one mentioned the gash on his chin or what happened with the pills.

Dez was in the halls between first and second period. Darren hadn't planned on stopping, but Dez's inquiring eyes made it tough not to. He stopped in front of Dez and they shook hands.

"What's up, Darren?"

"Nothing much, struggling with these classes."

Dez leaned in. "I heard about what went down."

"Where'd you hear?"

"Mike."

"You spreading it around these halls?"

"Nah."

"Not even to anyone on the team?"

"I wouldn't do that to you. No matter what's gone down in the past." Dez raised a fist and Darren pounded it.

"Yeah," Darren said.

"You need *anything*, you come to me, hear?" Dez said.

Darren wasn't used to *this* kind of attention, and it was hard to accept how things had changed. Before the shoulder injury, people at school had looked up to him. He had taken pressure off his teammates with his play and given hope to every student at Sunnyside that the team could be a winner. Darren was one of them; representing the hope that someone among them could rise up out of the Third Ward. Now, he was the one who needed hope. He wondered just how much Dez knew. Dez hadn't mentioned the pills outright, but if Dez had spoken to Mike, he probably knew it all.

Forget it. If he already knows, let me get some relief.

"There is something I need help with," Darren said. He rubbed his shoulder and winced. "My shoulder is killing me."

"They didn't give you anything for pain?" Dez asked.

"Just over-the-counter stuff," Darren said. "I could use something stronger."

Dez moved in closer. "Let me talk to some of the guys. There's always a painkiller or two floatin' around the locker room."

Darren nodded like an innocent child.

"But if I get them, you can't tell anybody that I gave them to you," Dez said, looking into Darren's eyes. "If Coach finds out, or your brother, I'm done."

"I got you."

"We're boys," Dez said, holding a fist up.

"Boys," Darren said, pounding Dez's fist with his left one.

"I'll check you later," Dez said and walked off.

As Darren entered into his second period classroom, a comfort washed over him. He couldn't believe his luck. It seemed that his teammates—aside from Dez—and the rest of school were in the dark about his incident, and now Dez was going to get him fixed up. The rest of the school day was a lot easier to get through because of the thought of those pills in his hand.

. . . .

Darren bumped into Dez at lunch and asked for an update. Dez said that he could get Darren some

Oxys from the team's starting tight end, Jeremiah Sweetney. Jeremiah was dealing with a badly sprained wrist and could spare a few pills for Darren.

Dez told Darren that he'd have the pills before practice.

Darren was cool with Jeremiah but didn't really know him outside of the locker room. The two used to go at each other pretty hard in practice, with Jeremiah not being the type to back down. Other than that, Darren knew Jeremiah to be a hardworking player who mostly kept to himself, similar to Darren with regards to his teammates. Darren did recall that Jeremiah was in fact dealing with a wrist problem, but had no inkling that he and Jeremiah had the same problem with the fat white pills.

. . . .

Darren didn't see Dez in the locker room before practice. His palms were sweating. He had a meeting with the trainer, and it wouldn't have been a good idea to show up late.

The trainer greeted Darren with a smile when he walked into the training room.

"How are you, Darren?" the trainer asked.

"Better. My shoulder is sore, but I'm getting used to it."

"I'm just gonna open up your bandage and take a look at the incision."

"A'ight."

The trainer unwrapped the bandage and removed the gauze over the incision.

"This looks like it's healing nicely," the trainer said.

Darren experienced no extreme pain in the shoulder, other than the general soreness that was to be expected.

The trainer straightened Darren's right arm and lifted it perpendicularly. Then he bent the arm at the elbow.

"Any pain?"

"Nah," Darren said.

"That's good," he said. "Really good. It's not ready to be rotated at the joint yet. But that's normal. Once the scar tissue starts coming in, you'll be ready to begin your rehab."

Darren watched the trainer as he spoke.

"I'd say two weeks, maybe ten days."

Darren made a fist with his right hand and the entire arm, from socket to fingertips, activated.

"Do you have any questions for me?"

Can you give me some damn Oxys?

"Questions?" Darren asked. "Nah, I'm straight."

"Okay, you're going to come back from this even stronger than before."

Darren smirked. *How do you know that?*

"We're gonna keep you going when things get tough with rehab."

"Thank you."

"Let me apply a new bandage."

The trainer redressed the wound with precision and delicacy. He replaced the sling and sent Darren on his way.

It was time for practice. But before heading out to the field, Darren spotted Dez getting dressed in front of his locker.

"You got 'em?"

"Yeah."

Dez looked around the locker room to make sure no one was watching. He reached into his locker and brought out a miniature Ziploc bag with five Oxys in it.

"Just five?"

"Yeah, nigga!" Dez said. "How many you need?"

"My bad." Darren slipped the baggie into his pocket.

Coach Adams smiled as he approached. "I'm glad to see you two patched things up," he said.

Both Darren and Dez smiled. Adams put his arm around Darren's good shoulder.

"Come on," he said. "I got a special job for you."

Marquis wasn't joking around when he said he'd be around more. He was standing on the sideline of Sunnyside's practice field, waiting for Darren to come out. Darren did a double take when he saw his older brother there. He couldn't remember the last time Marquis had come to one of his practices.

"What's up?" Marquis asked, as Adams and Darren approached.

"I'll give you two a few minutes," Coach Adams said.

Marquis reached out and gave his little brother a hug. He touched Darren's face like a father would a son. Darren couldn't remember one time in his life where Marquis had done that.

"How'd it go today?" Marquis asked.

Darren shrugged with a distant look in his eyes. He watched his teammates as they got loose before practice. Truth was, they didn't seem like teammates anymore. He was an outsider now, a spectator.

"This ain't right," Darren said, after a minute of brooding silence. "I don't belong out here like this."

Marquis smiled. "You know I thought the same, walking through those halls. But you can become someone new if you want to."

Darren watched his older brother with a careful eye, just to make sure he wasn't playing around. Marquis never talked this way.

Is he talking about leaving the dope game?

"Whatchu mean?"

"I don't know," Marquis said. "You think to yourself, 'Maybe I don't have to be one thing. Maybe I don't have to carry it a certain way.' Know what I mean?"

Darren didn't say anything. He put his hand in his pocket and dug around for the pills. He looked out as the team gathered at midfield.

"I don't know what I'm talking about," Marquis said.

Darren started laughing, and then Marquis joined in. The laughs were much needed after what the two brothers had been through recently.

Coach Adams walked over. "Marquis, I just wanted

to let you know that Boise State has promised to honor its scholarship offer if Darren takes his rehab serious *and* stays engaged with the team."

Marquis turned to Darren and smiled. "That's great news!" He turned back to Adams. "He's gonna do everything you ask of him, Coach Adams."

Coach Adams nodded and turned to Darren. "When we break up for individuals, I want you to come over and watch the d-line," he said.

"I can watch from here," Darren said.

"You're not a part of it over here," he said. "You have to be *on* the field with the guys."

"But I'm not a part of the team anymore," Darren said. "I can't do anything on the sidelines. I can't make plays. I sure as hell can't go to college by standing and watching."

Coach Adams glanced at Marquis, who had his hand on Darren's back.

"I'm nothing," Darren said. "I'm nothing standing over here."

"Just give it a try," Adams said. "I'm not here to

lie to you. I know it's hard for you, of all players to be standing over here. Think about it this way, if your teammates see you with them on the practice field they'll work that much harder."

"I'm not a cheerleader," Darren said.

"Nothing's gonna happen standing over here, feeling sorry for yourself," Marquis chimed in.

Darren looked down to the grass. This was too much for him.

"A'ight," Darren said. "Let me go use the bathroom and then I'll be over there."

"Okay," Adams said, before heading onto the field.

Darren turned for the locker room.

"Hold up, I'll come with you," Marquis said.

"What? You gonna watch me piss?" Darren said irritably.

"Nah. It's just that I know what you're going through right now."

"I told you, I'm done with all that."

"It ain't that simple, little brother."

"You don't believe me?"

"Honestly? I don't," Marquis said. "This is my business, D. Remember who you're talking to."

They walked to the bathroom, and when Darren tried to go into a stall, Marquis shook his head and motioned him to one of the open urinals. Marquis watched as Darren drained into a urinal. He had seen drug users take drugs in various ways over the years. It wouldn't have surprised him if his little brother tried to pop a pill right there and then.

Darren finished and washed his hands. Marquis was there waiting right as he turned around from the sink. "Damn!" Darren said. "Can I get a little privacy?"

"You got anything you want to give to me?"

"Huh?"

Marquis looked into Darren's eyes. Darren looked back with no hesitation. Marquis wasn't going to pat his brother down. He would rebuild the trust between them the right way by *being there* to watch over his little brother. A pat-down would destroy everything.

"Okay," Marquis said. "Get back on the field. Coach is waitin' on you."

14

THE PERSISTENT SOUND OF PADS POPPING RANG out as Darren joined his team on the practice field. The different position groups were going through their routines to get ready for the first game of the season. Darren liked practice. He wasn't a diva type who only gave it his all during games—instead, he gave everything he had at all times. This was one of the many reasons why Coach Adams had named Darren a team captain before his junior season. And as he watched Darren squirm on the sideline, he remembered how badly he had wanted Darren to become more of a vocal leader during this, his senior season.

"Hey Darren," Adams said, after walking over.

Darren nodded. The defensive line drills were going on behind Coach Adams. The players were working on their get-off after the football was snapped. The d-line coach, Coach Mustaine, was simulating the snap by hiking the ball to himself.

"Ready! Hut! Hut!" Coach Mustaine boomed, before another dry-snap.

The set of defensive linemen exploded off the ball.

"Good! Good!" Coach Mustaine said. "That's the kind of explosion I want!"

Darren looked on as his teammates went through the basic drill. He wasn't sure why Coach Adams wanted him out there. He wasn't adding anything to the team by watching. He could've just showed up to the games to remind Sunnyside's faithful that he was still alive and breathing. It was more irritating than anything else, to be this close to the action without being able to play.

The second string line was now ready to participate in the drill. Darren noticed one of the back-up defensive ends, a Third Ward kid named Jason, was lining up kind of funny. Jason's back foot was way too far back. *He'll never generate any power and speed like that.*

"Jason!" Coach Mustaine yelled. "What the hell was that? Is that the fastest you can go?"

Darren tapped Adams on the shoulder, and he turned around.

"His stance is wrong," Darren said.

"Who?"

"The sophomore, Jason."

"You think so?" Adams asked. He *knew* that all Darren Taylor needed was a spark—a curiosity—that would turn into something good.

"Yeah, if he closes his stance a little, he'll have more balance. More balance means more explosion."

"Okay. So go teach him the *right* way."

"Teach him what?"

"How to line up in a proper stance," Adams replied. "With you on the sideline, we need more pass rushers. Jason has raw talent, but he can't be out there with no technique."

"Coach . . . I . . . "

"Jason would appreciate it," Adams said. "I would too. And it can only make you better when you get back. Seeing the game from this angle."

Darren didn't respond. Coach Adams turned back to the drill and smiled again.

After a couple more basic drills, the defensive linemen took a water break. Darren hovered around the coolers, without interacting with his teammates. They were aware of his presence because injured or not, Darren was someone they looked up to and respected. And though rumors swirled, they would not hold what was being alleged against him.

Coach Mustaine came over and put an arm around Darren's good shoulder. Darren smiled. He liked Mustaine. They had engaged in many battles over Darren's two and a half seasons on varsity. Darren hadn't taken to Coach Mustaine's abrasive style of coaching at first, but after getting through the initial hurt pride, he realized that his d-line coach knew a lot about the game.

"Hey Darren," Mustaine said. "How's the shoulder?"

Coach Adams came jogging over from the quarterbacks' drills. He stopped in front of Coach Mustaine and Darren. He put his hand on Darren's back.

"I want to pull Jason out and have him work with Darren on the side," Adams said.

"He needs it," Mustaine said and looked over at Darren.

Darren turned to Adams. "I'm no coach."

"You know the game," Adams said.

"Jason!" Mustaine belted out. "Go over there with Darren. He's gonna teach you a thing or two about that shoddy first step of yours!"

The other defensive lineman laughed as Jason jogged over to where Darren and the coaches were. Coach Mustaine gave Jason a thump on the shoulder pad before rejoining the rest his charges.

"Jason, you know Darren," Adams said.

"Everyone does," Jason said. His eyes were open and accepting, as he stood next to one of his Third Ward idols—Darren, who had avoided the corners and made something positive out of himself.

Darren nodded and the two shook.

"He's gonna work with you a little bit," Adams said.

"Cool," Jason said.

"I'll leave you guys to it," Adams said, before jogging over to the linebackers.

The rest of the defensive lineman circled around Coach Mustaine and readied for their next drill—one-on-ones with the offensive line. Darren watched his d-line mates go to work. For a moment, he forgot about Jason standing next to him. Darren shook his head, and after catching a glimpse of Jason out of the corner of his eye, turned to face him.

"Come on," Darren said. "Let's go over here."

The two of them walked over to an open space on the sideline.

"A'ight, get down in a stance," Darren said.

Jason got down in his unorthodox, splay-limbed stance, and up close, the sight of it made Darren laugh.

"What?" Jason asked self-consciously.

"How you expect to rush like that?" Darren asked. "Look at how far back your right foot is."

Jason stood up. "I've always lined up like that."

"Well it's wrong," Darren said. "You do that up at this level, them big tackles will toss you around."

I'm not a coach. Who am I kidding?

A sadness fell over Darren and though not out of spite, once again he turned his back on Jason. For his part, Jason waited patiently, ready to listen to anything Darren had to say about playing defensive end. Darren again watched the rest of the defensive linemen with Coach Mustaine and after a little while, Jason watched too. Coach Mustaine was a wild man when he was out on the field, always at high volume, sweating more than any person should. But there was a passion bursting out of him. Anybody could see it. That passion was what Darren responded to. It's what all Sunnyside's defensive linemen responded to.

"A'ight," Darren said. "Get down in your funky-ass stance again."

Jason smiled and got down. This time, Darren got down into a three-point stance with him. The right shoulder was stiff, but there was no pain. Darren put his right foot back and left hand into the dirt.

"See, if you can tighten up your stance a little," Darren said.

He mimicked coming off the ball at the snap. Although the action looked clunky because of the right arm in the sling, Jason saw the potential in the adjustment. Darren reset and fired off the ball again. Jason watched and then got down in a stance. This time, he cut down the distance between his legs. He fired out of his stance and the difference was plain to see.

"See, there you go," Darren said, with a smile. "There you go."

"Yeah, it's better. I can tell," Jason said.

"Just keeping working until it comes natural."

"Anything else?" Jason asked.

"Yeah, bury that stance you were using before."

The two of them laughed and shook hands. Darren put his left hand on Jason's shoulder, and it wasn't until a few seconds later that he caught himself. *Damn. I just taught this fool something.*

"Yo, D, you mind teaching me some of your pass-rush moves?" Jason asked.

"Get the stance down first and we'll talk."

· ·

Marquis met Darren after practice, and the two of them got into the Expedition. Darren had forgotten all about the Oxys in his pocket until his butt hit the passenger seat. He rested his left hand across his right pocket where the pills were stashed.

"How'd it go out there today? Marquis asked.

Darren shrugged. "It was okay."

"That boy Jason got any game?"

"I guess we'll find out Friday night."

"I'll be there."

Marquis's phone buzzed in the center console. He ignored it.

"You're gonna go to the game, even though I'm not playing?" Darren said. "I can't count all the games you've missed before. Games where I played like a beast."

A moment passed before Marquis could gather his thoughts. His phone buzzed again. The calls and texts from Mike were relentless. This time Marquis looked at his phone and sighed.

"I know I haven't been the best brother. And I'm sorry about that. But I'm trying to be better. I really am. I want you to know that. I'm trying to be a better person for you, Mom, and myself."

"Right," Darren said, with his mind on the drugs in his pocket.

Marquis looked over at his younger brother and then back to the road. His phone kept buzzing until they reached home. Marquis parked the truck out in front and Darren unbuckled his seatbelt. Though he turned off the ignition, Marquis stayed buckled. Darren looked over with questioning eyes.

"I'm gonna make a call and then be in."

Darren nodded.

"Is there any food in there?" Marquis asked.

Darren shook his head.

"Order a couple of pizzas."

Darren exited the truck and walked inside the house. Marquis pulled out his phone and scanned over the cache of missed calls and texts from his number two. Something was up. He scrolled through the list of recently dialed numbers and hit call. The phone rang a couple of times before a voice on the other end picked up.

"Can I talk to the nurse Sadie, please?"

Marquis waited as the other person spoke.

"Tell her it's Marquis Taylor . . . Okay, I'll hold."

Marquis waited three minutes until Sadie picked up the line."

"Marquis?"

Her voice was harried.

"Sadie," he said. "Sorry to bother."

"Everything alright with Darren?"

"Darren. Yeah. He's fine. At the moment."

She sighed impatiently on the other end.

"Look, I was just calling because I needed someone to talk to. I don't know—I don't really have anyone else. Can I meet up with you tomorrow morning? We could have breakfast or something?"

There was a pause on the line.

"How about tonight?" she replied. "But it's not a date, okay? Just to talk, like you said."

Marquis stayed silent.

"I get off in two hours."

Sadie's sureness was a foreign idea to Marquis. The females he dealt with were the opposite.

"Alright. Yeah. Tonight."

"Meet me out in front of the hospital," she said. "There's a quiet place there we can talk."

"Okay."

"See you later," she said before hanging up.

Marquis pressed *end*.

Mike sent another text.

where u at? Call me . . . it's gettin wild out here.

Another one came:

AND I found the dudes 'sponsible 4 darren.

Marquis didn't respond to either of the texts. He got out of the truck and walked inside the house. Darren was in the living room when Marquis walked in. They exchanged glances before Marquis walked upstairs to check on their mother. Darren hadn't taken the pills while Marquis was out in the car because he knew his older brother was watching him close. He'd have his chance when Marquis had to go out to take care of something for work.

Marquis walked back downstairs.

"I ordered two pizzas," Darren said. "One with grilled chicken for me and the other, pepperoni."

Marquis nodded and took out a fifty-dollar bill from a roll in his pocket. He placed the bill on the dining room table.

"This place is a mess," Marquis said. He started

to collect empty bottles and old food containers lying around the kitchen, dining room and living room. He filled two garbage bags and set them in the cans in the front yard. He walked back into the house and eyed Darren, who was sitting on the couch and watching TV.

"What?"

"You got homework?" Marquis asked.

"Yeah."

Marquis grabbed the remote and turned off the TV. "So do it before the food gets here."

Darren looked at his older brother like he had lost it. But the truth was, Marquis's newfound attention and concern made Darren happy. Instead of protesting, he grabbed his backpack and started with his government class.

Marquis set out to clean the kitchen. His phone buzzed periodically, though he ignored all the messages and calls. He washed a pile of dishes that were in the sink, then he wiped the counters and stove, and disinfected the inside of the fridge. He opened all of the cupboards and made a pile of all the stuff that had gone bad. He bagged those up and put them out front in the cans. When Marquis walked back in, he stopped in front of the couch again. Darren had finished his government homework and was onto English.

"This ain't right with Mom," Marquis said.

"It's how she is," Darren said.

"Still ain't right."

There was a knock at the door—the pizza had arrived. Marquis nodded to the kitchen.

"Take out some plates and napkins. I'll go shopping tomorrow. Get some real food up in here."

Darren smiled. He was excited to be sharing a meal with just his older brother.

15

AFTER DINNER, MARQUIS CLEANED UP A LITTLE more, checked on his mother again, and then went out to meet to Sadie. Before leaving, he went out to his truck and grabbed a duffel bag of clothes. He brought the bag into the house and dropped it on the living room floor. He wanted Darren to see that they were in this together. No shortcuts.

Darren responded not with words, but a true smile—one that wasn't forced or induced by something football-related. He continued with his homework, forgetting again about the pills in his pocket.

In the car, Marquis thought about calling Mike, but the urge to talk to Sadie first proved too strong. She seemed to have a calming effect on both him and Darren. He *knew* her even though they had never met before Darren's string of hospital visits. This feeling was strong inside of Marquis, though they hadn't even talked much when he was at Darren's side in the hospital.

Marquis parked his truck in the hospital's main lot, and Sadie was out front to meet him, looking exhausted. She smiled at him upon sight. Even in her scrubs she looked good. Marquis smiled back and tried not to be brash about it.

"The benches are over here," she said.

They walked over to a small picnic area that was offset from the main entrance. Sadie crossed her legs as she sat at one of the tables. Marquis sat down next to her, leaving a little space between them. Her eyes were heavy. Marquis didn't want to waste her time.

"Thanks for meeting me," he said. "I know nurses

work hard. You're probably tired and want to go home already."

"Don't worry about it," she said. "I was concerned about Darren."

He smiled. "This ain't about Darren, though." Marquis sighed and interlocked his fingers. He looked out to the parking lot before turning back to Sadie.

"I'm not used to this," he said. "I don't know if I've ever talked to someone. I mean, really talk. I'm not even sure I know how to do it."

"You're doing it now."

"This thing with my brother. It shook me."

Sadie nodded.

"Seeing you, I mean, you're someone who is this really good person that helps people. And I'm— well, I . . . " He trailed off for a moment, "I want to change, but to tell you the truth, I don't know where to begin."

Sadie watched him with eyes that now weren't quite so tired.

"I want to change." Marquis took a deep breath

and closed his eyes. He let the cool night air touch his skin. He opened his eyes back up and looked over at Sadie.

"I . . . " he said before pausing. "I'm a drug dealer."

Sadie's face did not change; no judgements passed.

"I've been a drug dealer since, since forever. Since I was a kid. Now you can't get drugs in the Third Ward without them coming from me. You can't sell drugs without my permission. That's . . . "

He paused again and looked down at the sidewalk between his shoes. The moon was out in full, silvery, like it had been hand polished.

"That's me," he said.

She still didn't speak. Something inside told her that he still needed to talk. She was there to listen.

"And I can't get the thoughts out of my head, like, did all this happen because of me? I don't know. Did my brother get hooked on pills because of me? Did he almost get killed trying to cop these *pills* because of me? Is my mom an alcoholic because of me? Do you think I'm being punished for what I've done?"

"If you want the truth, I'll give it to you," she said softly. "Do I think that someone, God or whoever, is punishing you because of your past?"

Marquis waited for her answer.

"No, I don't think that," she said. "But it is all connected. That I can say. Your brother has to be carrying a lot of pain because of who you are. It hasn't caught up to Darren until now because of his injury. I bet being your brother is hard for him, though. I know who you are, Marquis."

"You do?"

"I don't mean that I've seen you around town or even heard your name before. I *know* you from seeing you in here with Darren lately. I know you can't be all bad. I see how you are with your brother. Now, I see that you want to change."

"What should I do?" Marquis asked, interlocking his hands again.

"If you need someone to tell you to quit selling drugs," she said, "I can't be that person. I can't tell you how to live."

Marquis watched Sadie in silence.

"But what I can do is share some of my pain with you."

Her eyes began to water. She blew a deep breath out between tightly puckered lips. The thing she was about to share with Marquis was something from her past. She hadn't thought about it in a long time, and it took her years to bury it. All of this with Darren had pushed it to the forefront again and her shared experience with Marquis—though hers was charged with much more emotion—was the only reason she sat on that bench.

"My brother was in the game. He lived by it. All of it. I won't tell you his name, but you probably knew him. I know he was violent. I saw him beat up a boy really bad one time over twenty dollars."

Sadie's eyes narrowed to another place, that old carousel of pain, anger, confusion, and devastation in her head, where her brother still had a shot to be something other than what he was.

Marquis dipped his head and did everything he

could to fight his own tears from flowing. He knew how this story would end.

"My brother was shot and killed in the Third Ward. I was on a training shift in this hospital when the EMTs wheeled him in with a gunshot wound to the chest. I wasn't even a full-fledged nurse yet. He died in front of me. I was too frozen to work on him. They couldn't stop the bleeding."

Marquis put his hand on her back. Tears began to flow down her cheeks.

"I didn't say anything to him. He was past words. But we stared at each other before he died. That'll stay with me."

Sadie stood up from the bench and wiped her eyes. She picked her car keys out of her purse.

Marquis stood as well.

"Anytime you're thinking about putting drugs out in the neighborhood, or anywhere in Houston, think about Darren and the other young brothers out here like him."

Marquis was silent.

"Also, you could think of me," she said, before walking away.

. . . .

Darren finished his homework right before the pain in his right shoulder returned. He tried to will it out of his mind, but the constant, rhythmic throbbing was too much to bear. He pulled the ziplock baggie from his pocket—containing the same pills that, when first received earlier that day, represented a formality rather than a simple choice. It was a choice now. His shoulder was causing him pain. *What am I gonna do?*

There wasn't much danger in it. Marquis was out, and if he returned anytime soon, Darren's narcotic aloofness could've easily been pawned off as sleepiness from a long first day back at school and practice. *Just one more time—or maybe not. I have Marquis here with me now. Really, with me. He'll help me through this. But the pain . . .*

Darren shifted the ziplock between his fingers. Surprisingly, it wasn't Marquis or Coach Adams that popped into his mind. He didn't fret over letting the two of them down. It was Jason that flashed through. He thought about the way Jason looked up to him. It was the same way he looked up to Marquis.

He got up off the couch and walked over to Marquis's duffel bag. He dropped the ziplock baggie on top of the duffel bag and walked into the kitchen to drink a full glass of water because he remembered Sadie telling him that dehydration was the main culprit that brought on the stiffening discomfort. He walked upstairs, and after checking up on his mother, went into his room, shut the door and got into bed.

. . . .

A few minutes after his meeting with Sadie, Marquis started up his truck and left the hospital. When his phone rang again, he answered it, finally taking a call from Mike. He thought about the sureness of Sadie's words as Mike yelled something in his ear.

"Yo! I got these niggas right now!" Mike screamed. "The ones who rolled Darren!"

"Where?" Marquis said, reverting to instinct.

"I got them here with some muscle. By the railroad tracks. Waitin' on you."

"Be right there. Don't do anything without me."

Marquis hung up and gunned the truck. He reached under his seat and clutched his favorite gun, the nine millimeter, also out of reflex.

．．．．．．．．．．．．．．．．．．．．．．．．．．．．

The old railroad tracks on the edge of the Third Ward were long defunct, a place deserted enough to get revenge. Marquis skidded to a stop right in front of four men, two of whom were on their knees. The two standing men were Mike and their crew's most reliable muscle, Domino. Both Mike and Domino held semi-automatics on the other two men. On closer inspection, they were not men at all. They were Darren's age.

The tall one was bloodied up something fierce and the short one wasn't too far behind. Their faces held resignation over the inevitable.

"These them?" Marquis demanded. "These sorry-looking niggas."

The instinct fermented inside Marquis, and with it came the fuzzy—almost narcotic-like—sensation of invincibility. Instead of existing solely inside the fugue state, like he had in the past, Marquis *recognized* the urge.

"Yeah," Mike said. "I know you said to call off the manhunt, but I knew your head was all jacked up at the time. I knew to keep looking."

Marquis nodded.

"Here they are," Mike said.

Marquis took a step toward the two boys. In the past, he'd have just pulled the trigger and ended the drive for retribution, painlessly and without comment. But perhaps *this* was change? An increment of change, at least. For once, Marquis thought before lifting his nine millimeter.

"Why'd you do it?"

The two boys looked to each other in suspense; though not because of the outcome that was staring them in the face. It was just that here they were about to get it, and Marquis Taylor was speaking to them.

"Uh," the tall one stammered.

"Why'd you beat and rob my little brother?"

"We didn't know it was D, and if we did, it would've never gone down like it did."

The response, though steeped in truth, enraged Marquis, and he responded with action rather than words. He took out his gun, turned off the safety, and steadied it in the tall one's face.

"Wait!" the tall one screamed. "It was a mistake! We'd never cross you like that. You the king of this here!"

Marquis took a deep breath. The barrel was pointed straight at the tall one's chin, in the same spot he had pistol-whipped Darren. The irony was lost on Marquis. This choice was not a hard one. Marquis had killed before and for offenses that were far less egregious. These boys meant nothing to him. His hand did not shake with his finger on the trigger. The tall boy closed his eyes because he knew what came next. He opened his eyes and looked up to Marquis.

Marquis clicked on the safety. He raised the gun and backed away.

"Cut them loose," Marquis said to Mike, who was behind him.

"Huh?"

"Just do it."

Marquis put the nine millimeter into his waist-band and got into his truck before driving away. A few blocks down the road, he dropped his beloved gun into a storm drain.

. . . .

After Marquis walked inside his mother's house, he

bent down to pick up his duffel bag. He noticed a ziplock bag holding five pills. They were Oxys. He looked around the living room like there was an intruder in the house. But he knew how the pills got there. When the pang of shock wore off, there was no anger behind it. *This* actually encouraged Marquis. The war wasn't over by any means, but at least Darren proved that he could survive a battle on his own.

Marquis flushed the pills in the downstairs toilet, drank a full glass of water, and grabbed his duffel bag before going upstairs to sleep. He checked on his mother and brother before going into his old room. Marquis hadn't slept in his old room in close to ten years. He walked inside and dropped his bag on the floor. He got into bed thinking like it would be one of those nights where sleep would be hard to come by. He was wrong. Everybody in the house was safe. Marquis closed his eyes and slept like a baby.

16

MARQUIS WOKE UP EARLY AND HELPED HIS MOTHER out of bed. She didn't want to get up but her oldest son had insisted. He walked her downstairs, and remembering that there was no food in the fridge to make breakfast, ran out to the corner store up the block for some essentials. A few corner boys who were up early marveled at the sight of Marquis Taylor jetting in and out of the liquor store with a loaf of white bread, instant coffee, orange juice, eggs, milk, and cereal. Marquis paid them no mind because he was intent on getting home quick. He didn't want his mother getting back into bed.

When he returned, his mother was still downstairs and awake. Marquis made coffee and then eggs—scrambled for him and Darren, sunny-side up for her. His mother ate and drank with contentedness on her face, as if eggs and coffee mixed together formed an elixir potion that would bring her back to life. Darren awoke and joined his family downstairs. It was a sideways picture: the three of them all up in the morning, together, eating a proper breakfast.

"Get some of these eggs in you," Marquis said, holding a spatula.

Darren fixed himself a plate of eggs and toast, along with a bowl of cereal. He washed it all down with two glasses of orange juice.

"I forgot the boy can eat," Marquis said.

"He's big," their mother said, putting a hand to Darren's cheek. Her eyes were clear, the fog knocked out of them by real food and good vibes.

Darren finished and went upstairs to get changed for school. Marquis sat while his mother enjoyed another cup of coffee. The silence between them, that normal morning silence that many families experience, was a welcome thing for Marquis and his mother. For many years their standard interaction was some variation of Marquis getting angry about her drinking then leaving, and she drinking even more as a result. *This* was okay though. Both Marquis and his mother could get used to it.

Marquis finished cleaning and went upstairs to shower and change clothes. After getting out of the shower, he caught a look of himself in the bathroom mirror. His eyes looked different—the edges were softer now, the whites more visible. Whereas before, on the streets, his eyes held a sharp quality that if pushed too far, the result could be grave. He didn't need to have that look on his face anymore. Not at home. Not anywhere else. Marquis didn't know if this change would last. There was no way he could know because it was all new to him.

The ride to Sunnyside—like the morning as a whole—was uneventful. Marquis and Darren appreciated the calm. Marquis didn't need to talk to Darren about the pills he had left on his gym bag. No words could express the relief Marquis experienced with his brother taking this step. As far as where Darren got the pills, Marquis knew how and where to get that answer without asking Darren anything. He had a meeting with Mike after dropping Darren off at school.

When Marquis pulled up to Sunnyside, he and Darren exchanged knowing glances. Marquis put a hand on Darren's neck. Darren unbuckled his seatbelt and got halfway out of the truck.

"I'll see you out there before practice, hear?" Marquis said.

"A'ight."

Darren got out and walked toward the front entrance of school. He caught up with some friends before entering. Marquis's phone rang.

"Hello?"

"Yes, Mr. Adams. I wanted to check in on our deal," the insurance man said.

"Yeah," Marquis said. He caught another look at

Darren before he and his friends walked into school. His little brother's smile was as wide as he had ever seen it. "You know what? Forget about our deal. I changed my mind. My little brother is going to college. He don't need insurance for that. Send me a bill for your man's work."

As Marquis pulled away from school, he was thinking that this was his moment. This was the time that he could get it all right.

. . . .

Mike would meet Marquis at their usual spot, the place where they had met since the beginning. They dreamed of getting out of the Third Ward one day, not understanding that they could never fully get out. Mike sat in a car, sipping that morning's second round of lean out of an extra-large Styrofoam cup. The morning was cool, and Mike had all windows down. The birds were out in full effect. Their chirping painted the scene behind the abandoned church.

Marquis pulled up, put his truck into park and got out. Mike put his cup down in the car's cup holder and followed suit in exiting his car with a fraction of Marquis's intensity. They shook hands and embraced first. Mike was dipped in codeine, in slow motion, and Marquis eyed him with curiosity.

"What's up, boss?" Mike asked. "Last night was . . . crazy."

"I'm not your boss anymore, Mike," Marquis said.

"Whatchu' mean?"

"I'm out. I wanted to come here and tell you that in person because I owe you that. We've been through too much not to give you that."

Mike's eyes dropped, and he wiped the top of his scalp with a clumsy half-motion of his hand.

"Past this. I don't owe you anything else. It's yours if you want it. The Third Ward. The connect. All of it." Marquis chuckled. "You can even take over the note on my condo. I'm putting it up for sale if you don't want it."

"Word?" Mike said. "Hold up. You love that

place. That was the proudest I ever saw you when you bought it. You just gonna give all this up?"

"I got to."

"What are you gonna do?"

"Not this."

"So it's all mine?"

"If you want it," Marquis said.

Mike nearly fell flat on his face in his happy stupor, but caught himself. Marquis knew what the score was.

"I ain't here to preach to you about getting out too."

"Me?" Mike said. "Nah. I'd die without this."

"That's what I thought too. But I ain't dead . . ." Marquis stopped himself and smiled. "Sorry."

"You sure about this? After how hard we fought for everything?"

"I'm sure."

The two friends shook hands and half-hugged again.

"There is one thing you could do for me," Marquis said. "Like a parting gift."

"Anything."

"I need to know how these Oxys are getting into Sunnyside. Darren had some on him yesterday, and I know damn sure he didn't cop them from the hospital."

Mike shifted his stance, but this time the action was voluntary and completed with a cool precision. His eyes perked up too, before averting Marquis's stare. "Aw, you know 'Quis, that's not really my specialty."

Marquis held his stare, and finally, Mike met it.

"I move a little Oxy at Sunnyside," Mike admitted with a shrug. "What can I say? I'm an en-tre-per-nur."

Marquis couldn't help but laugh at Mike's stumble on the big word. He quickly became stone-faced again. "I hear you. But I need you to stop."

Mike didn't need long to think it over. He nodded solemnly.

"Thanks," Marquis said.

He turned around and started for his truck. There was one more thing. He turned back to face Mike.

"Who's pushing the Oxys for you at Sunnyside?"

"Truth?" Mike said.

"You always give me the truth. That's why we made a good team."

"Someone on the team."

"Dez?"

"Nah, I wouldn't put my little brother's neck out there like that."

"Who then?"

Mike took a deep breath. "You're killin' me with this parting gift."

Marquis held firm.

"Tight end," Mike said distantly. "Boy by the name of Jeremiah. Jeremiah Sweetney."

"Thanks, Mike. Oh, and if you can, stop moving Oxys at *all* the schools in Houston."

"I'm not hearing you anymore, 'Quis," Mike said. "One parting gift."

Marquis nodded and started for his truck. There

was *one* more thing. "Yo, Mike. I think you need to get help for your problem."

"Problem?"

"Yeah. With the *sizzurp*. The *lean*. *Purp*. Whatever you want to call it."

Mike flashed a sheepish grin. Marquis closed his eyes and took a deep breath. He opened them and considered his friend, then nodded.

"It's alright," Marquis said. "This is from one friend to another. If you ever need help kickin' that to the curb, you know my number."

"I got it under control, 'Quis," Mike said.

"That's fine," Marquis said. "But don't let these little players around the way see you drinkin' that stuff. Don't glamorize it."

Mike nodded.

Marquis got into his car and drove by his old friend with the window down. Mike approached.

"Take care of yourself, Mike."

"You too." Mike reached in the window to shake hands one last time.

Mike watched the Expedition pull away until it was out of sight. He stayed in the back parking lot of the church for a while, thinking on old times. He remembered that first summer when he and Marquis were little snot-nosed corner boys and a hundred degrees every day. They had a daily contest to see who could sell the most dimes. He thought, too, about that night seven years ago when they dropped their first bodies.

17

DARREN WALKED THROUGH SUNNYSIDE'S HALLS long before first bell and with all of his homework done for the first time in, well, forever. Homework was never a priority with football taking up so much time and energy. Now, this was just a regular old Thursday for Darren, without the pressure of performing under the Friday night lights. He could give a little extra attention to homework.

He was relaxed too. Though it wasn't that football created extra stress. It was often the opposite: a pressure release for whatever was going on in his real life. Darren was content to let his teammates carry it for a while. On the way to first period, he smiled at a couple of fine-looking girls he had never noticed in school before. They smiled back. He realized then that even without football, each day might bring a valuable and mysterious opportunity to learn something new. He had more than enough proof now. Just the day before, he found out that he could coach—a little at least—and that he could stay clean for a day, even though both achievements had seemed impossible. Now if he could only stay clean two days in a row.

* *

Lunch had arrived and Darren was in line to get food. Jason, the precocious sophomore defensive end, came up from behind and gave Darren a tap on his good shoulder. Darren turned and saw his understudy.

"What's up Jason?"

"Just wanted to get up with you and pay my respects again," Jason said. "For yesterday."

"You don't have to keep thanking me. It's cool."

"Okay."

Jason lingered next to Darren in line.

"Is there anything else I can help you with?" Darren asked.

Jason looked around the cafeteria before speaking.

"I gotta get at you," Jason said.

"Speak fool!"

"Not in here."

Darren looked into the underclassman's eyes, and it was the first time he saw something other than immaturity in them. These eyes were focused and serious. Darren thought back to his own early ascension up to varsity.

"Coach Adams said I had focused eyes when he decided to move me up to varsity," Darren said.

"Huh?"

"Never mind."

Jason looked around the cafeteria nervously as a group of corner-boys from the Third Ward walked in with a group of girls. Darren knew them as minor

dealers around the Third Ward and had no beefs—
that he knew of—with any of them. But he also did
not call any of them friends.

"Meet me in room two ten after I get my food,"
Darren said, staring at the corner-boys.

Jason walked past the group without looking at
them. They stared at him as he left the cafeteria. After
buying a turkey sandwich and two mini-cartons of
whole milk, Darren walked past the group and looked
at each of its male members straight in his eyes.

Darren made his way to the second floor and
turned a corner to find the empty classroom. Jason
was inside, eating a candy bar and drinking a soda.

"Why'd you pick here?"

"Because it's empty," Darren said. "I come here
when I need to think. Usually on the day of a big
game."

Jason nodded and took a bite from his candy bar.

"I used to eat like that," Darren said.

"Like what?"

"Candy and soda."

Jason looked at the candy bar in his hand.

"If I were you, I would eat good before tomorrow night's game. You might actually play some meaningful snaps. The team we're playing throws a lot," Darren said. "Candy, soda. That don't help you get better. You need to put real food in your body."

Jason stood up and threw the other half of the candy bar and can of soda into the trashcan. He paced around the empty room, and Darren watched him as he took the first bite of his sandwich. After a little more of Jason's pacing, Darren couldn't take anymore.

"Stop!" Darren said. He put his sandwich down. "Why do you need to talk to me?"

Jason came over and spoke in a low voice. The precaution seemed silly to Darren at first, but then he remembered what it was like to be a sophomore on a team with mostly juniors and seniors.

"You know Jeremiah, right?"

"Yeah," Darren said.

"Jeremiah got expelled today," Jason said. "The

principal pulled him out of third period. The cops were waiting for him in the principal's office."

"Why?"

"They got him for dealing Oxys at school."

Darren froze for a second and then played it off.

"Why are you telling me this?"

Jason looked around again before speaking.

"Dudes around school are saying you snitched. Saying *you* were the one who put Coach Adams and the principal on Jeremiah."

"I ain't no snitch."

"That's what I been telling everybody," Jason said, with comfort. The young player took solace in the fact that Darren personally defended himself against the allegations.

"Anyone on the team saying that?"

"Nah," Jason said with conviction. "It's mostly them dudes we just saw in the cafeteria."

"I'll tell you what," Darren said. "You let all of them know—and I mean all of them—that if they think I'm snitching, they know where to find me."

Jason released a deep breath.

"They been giving you any trouble?" Darren asked.

Jason shrugged his shoulder. "Just talkin' and a few mean mugs. Nothing I can't handle."

"Oh yeah, I didn't see Dez in first period today. Is he talkin' about me?"

"Dez ain't come to school today."

It made sense. Dez was the one who got the pills from Jeremiah before giving them to Darren. Dez knew that Jeremiah was going to get busted. That's why he wasn't in school. Dez would never miss the Thursday practice before the first game of the season unless it was serious. And Dez's freedom being taken away rated as serious.

"A'ight," Darren said. "Thanks for this."

"No doubt."

Darren turned to leave.

"Darren," Jason said.

Darren turned around.

"I'll see you at practice after school, right?"

Darren thought for a moment and then smiled.

"Yeah, I'll see you out there. We got work to do for tomorrow night's game."

Jason smiled and Darren left the room. He walked down the empty hallway until it reached a dead end of three classrooms. Lunch period was almost over and Darren needed to think. Jeremiah could've ended his hopes of going to college right then if the tight end told that he supplied Dez Oxys to give to Darren. The bell rang and a minute later, a flood of sound made its way into the second floor hallway.

. . . .

Marquis sat in a cold, white office. It belonged to head narcotics detective of Houston's South Central Division, James "Jimi" Oatson. As a child, Oatson survived the Third Ward's toughest neighborhood—the cross of Dowling and McGowen—to join the police force, starting with patrol division, through a little stint downtown with homicide, and all the way full circle as head of narcotics in the Third Ward. He knew firsthand how damaging of a presence drugs were in the Third Ward. He also knew the man sitting in front of him was largely responsible.

"I'm not sure I fully understand," Oatson said, wetting his salt and pepper mustache between thoughts. His eyes questioned Marquis right along with his words.

"I mean what I said," Marquis said. "Every word."

"You're taking responsibility for the Oxycontin that is being spread around Sunnyside High School?"

Marquis nodded, looking into Oatson's hazel eyes.

"But why?"

"We already went through this Detective Oatson—"

"Call me Jimi."

"Okay, Jimi. *I* was the one who gave the pills to Sweetney. No one else from my crew has that kind of authority on pills. I'm the only one."

"And Sweetney then gave them to . . . " Oatson looked down to the notepad sitting atop his desk and read a name off of it. "Dez Harmon. Brother of your number two, Mike Harmon. That's interesting. And Dez finally passed them off to your little brother Darren. Is that all correct?"

"Yes."

Oatson closed the notepad. "You know how long I've been chasing you?"

"Nah."

"Too long."

Marquis didn't flinch.

"And to come in here like this and just give yourself up."

Oatson shook his head.

"Somethin' don't smell right," he said.

"It's pretty simple. I don't want my brother, or anyone else on his team, to take the fall for the pills. Because I'm the one who put them in those halls."

"I don't doubt that you've put a lot drugs into the halls of our schools in the Third Ward. And God knows what other schools and neighborhoods in Houston. It's just that I doubt your motive here. This doesn't feel right. You know the rules better than anyone. You know that pills are federal territory. That can put you away for a long time on the first hit."

Marquis fixed his mouth to speak again and then closed it.

"You want to know what I think?" Oatson asked.

Marquis shrugged.

"I think that your little errand boy, Mike, was the one who put them pills in Sweetney's hands. And you're taking the fall for your little brother. So he doesn't get hurt."

"No," Marquis said, stone-faced. "*I'm* the one who put those pills in those halls. Me. No one else."

Oatson sat for a while, transfixed on Marquis Adams. He understood what was happening. He just could not understand *how* it was happening. How could someone who had spilled so much blood in a community and spread heroin and cocaine like a disease, just give it all up? Sure, Oatson had seen his share of "turnarounds," but they were usually much older. As recent as a week ago, Marquis was entrenched as the owner of the most prosperous territory in the Third Ward. And to just let that all go? Oatson had to know why. He opened his mouth to ask the question, but something in Marquis's face stopped him. There was a calm and relief in this young man's eyes sitting across from him. And that calmness stifled Oatson.

"We done here?" Marquis asked.

Oatson snapped out of his daze.

"Done?" Oatson asked.

"Yeah."

Oatson stood up from his desk.

"Yes. We can wrap it up from here. You're gonna need to call your lawyer and—"

"No lawyers," Marquis said. "I'm ready."

"You're gonna go away for a long ride."

"I'm good with it."

"Okay."

"Just one thing?"

"Tell me what it is, and I'll tell you if I can do it for you."

"Drive me over to Sunnyside," Marquis said.

18

MARQUIS SAT IN THE PASSENGER SEAT OF Oatson's Caprice Classic. They drove through the Third Ward in silence mostly. The only sound came from Oatson sighing heavily when they drove through the carnage of his old neighborhood.

As they neared Sunnyside High School, Oatson finally came out with it. "You know, I've been waiting a long time to bust you," he said. "Dreaming of it. I've come closer than you'd ever know." Oatson's chest was puffed out as he steered with both hands.

"We've had hard evidence of your organization's drug-dealing in the Third Ward, and we've had twenty something bodies linked to you," Oatson continued.

Marquis looked out the window at the Third Ward.

"But we could never get a witness to testify," the detective said, without the slightest hint of anger or disgust. "Not one witness."

"I've been thinking on this the last few days," Marquis said finally. "I'm giving it back. No, not giving it back. There's no way I could ever give it all back. There's too much blood and not enough time. I'm just tryin'. Tryin' to do it the other way."

"It ain't really fair this way," Oatson said. "The good guys are supposed to bust the bad guys. You're a bad guy."

"All I know, is I'm here and I'm ready to carry it. All of it. I'll do the time."

"Ain't right," Oatson said. "I get what you're doing, but you won't hear me thank you. And I can't absolve you. You going away may help—but it won't make it all right. That's between you and The Almighty."

The Third Ward passed by the two men. The place they both once called home was losing one of its sons to a familiar fate. There was a saying in the Third Ward that as a male, you either left the easy way or the hard way. Dead was the easy way. You died a soldier's death, and if there was an afterlife, the man upstairs would overlook your bad deeds as simple soldiering. The hard way was prison.

Marquis said goodbye to the Third Ward in his head. He thought about his mother and the pain this would bring her, and for a heartbeat he thought of reaching over, grabbing Oatson's glock, and going out the easy way.

· ·

Darren waited for something to happen the rest of the day at school. He waited for a call from Marquis. He waited to be summoned to Coach Adams's office and then the principal's. He waited for a hallway confrontation with one of the corner-boys from the

Third Ward. None of it came. He went into the locker room after school, and the happenings inside were mostly routine. Dez and Jeremiah were not there, but other than that, the rest of the players on the team were getting ready for the final practice before the first game of the season. The brisk, forty-five-minute walkthrough practice called for the team to dress in "shells"—helmets and shorts—in an effort to avoid injury. As far as Darren knew, he would still be working with Jason to get him ready for his first game at the varsity level.

He dropped his backpack in his locker and took a seat. He looked around for Jason, but couldn't find him. An inspection of the sophomore's locker revealed that he was already dressed and out on the field. *Good. The boy's hungry.* Darren smiled at the thought and then noticed that he was all alone in the locker room. The place was silent.

There was uncertainty surrounding the team. Darren had no idea about his future. He wasn't sure if it would all come crashing down—college, health, life. There was no guarantee that any of it would work out to where he could just play ball again. What he did know was that he had not taken a single pill in a few days, and if it took all this to keep him clean—getting pills secretly from teammates, hiding them, and deciding at the last minute not to take them—he'd never make it that long again. He knew if he wanted to stay clean, he'd have to cut the pills out of his life completely, on his own.

He left the locker room and walked onto the field for practice.

Marquis, sitting in Oatson's parked Caprice at the edge of the lot near Sunnyside's practice field, watched for his little brother to emerge. Darren came out of the locker room—frowning—and slowly joined the rest of his stretching teammates on the field, though he didn't interact with anyone.

"There he is," Oatson said.

"Okay," Marquis said, as he exited the Caprice. He turned around and stared at Oatson through the open passenger window. "Meet me out front in ten minutes."

He went into the school.

. . . .

"Why are you smiling?" Adams asked.

Marquis sat before Coach Adams, in his office, about five minutes before the start of practice.

"Nothing," Marquis said in reply.

"I never thought it would happen like this," Adams said. "You and me working together. I used to always worry about my Third Ward kids working *for* you." He smiled, but the expression did nothing to cover the utter confusion that painted the rest of his face.

"I know where Jeremiah got the pills," Marquis said. "I don't want anything to happen to him."

"Is that because you want to protect Jeremiah, or because you want to protect Darren?"

"Don't ask."

Coach Adams raised his arms in surrender. "You're right. I don't want to know."

Marquis stood up. "I want to make sure Darren keeps his scholarship. He worked his ass off for it, and I'll be damned if he loses it because of me."

Coach Adams was frozen as if he was watching his own dream.

"Can you promise me that Darren will keep his scholarship to Boise State?" Marquis asked.

"Last I heard from the assistant up there, the one who recruited Darren, was that if Darren takes his rehab seriously, Boise State will honor its offer."

Marquis sat back down.

"But being charged with possession of prescription painkillers, even if it's just a rumor, will not look good. I've seen schools pull scholarship offers for less."

"Darren just had major surgery," Marquis said. "That's explains the painkillers right there."

"Yeah, but this thing with Jeremiah and Dez. If it gets out, and it will, Boise State will have second thoughts."

Marquis was silent.

"And you being who you are, doesn't help Darren," Adams said.

Marquis put his face in his hands and rubbed his eyes. Aside from everything else, he was exhausted too. His life—the time spent, all those years doing dirt, and even the last few days spent doing the right thing—all of it, was catching up to him.

"You'll tell the cops who supplied Jeremiah with the Oxys?" Adams asked.

"Yes."

"You'll go away for a long time."

"Let me deal with that," Marquis said.

Marquis stood. Coach Adams stood too, and the two men shook hands.

"I could've done more," Adams said, shaking his head.

"I'm gonna make this right," Marquis said.

Marquis left Adams's office, and exited Sunnyside through the front door for the first time since his short-lived stint as a student there.

19

SUNNYSIDE'S PRACTICE FIELD WAS EERIE IN ITS hushed tone. Maybe it was quiet because Dez wasn't out there talking his usual smack. That was part of it, but not all. The team was mainly subdued because they had been through a lot during the preseason, from the injury to Darren, to the incident with Dez and Jeremiah. The game itself takes so much focus and concentration that it makes it almost impossible to win when there are things to contend with that are *outside* the white lines.

Darren was standing on the edge of a defensive line drill, and Coach Mustaine was hammering the guys with comments that were two-thirds motivational and one-third profane. At a water break, Mustaine walked over to Darren.

"How's the wing?" he asked.

Darren looked down at his right arm in its sling. "I'm not thinking about the pain anymore," he said. "I guess that's something."

"It is."

"I want to walk off, Coach."

"You mean off the practice field?"

"No. I mean for good."

"Darren, it's been easy for you so far. I mean on the field. But it ain't always gonna be easy. You're good enough to make it to the NFL. Trust me. I've seen guys that had what it took. And you have it. Your first setback and you wanna walk? You're way stronger than that. You gotta show some resiliency, son."

Darren had heard all this before. He *had* faced adversity, growing up in the Third Ward without a father. But playing ball in college—let alone the

NFL—wasn't his clear-cut destiny. The thought of getting to play again was distant, phantasmal, and Coach Mustaine's motivation rang hollow.

"One thing I've never seen," Coach Mustaine said, with his right pointer finger in the air, "and I don't care how much talent you have. I never saw a player make it far without experiencing adversity *on* the field."

A horn sounded in the distance, signifying the end of the break. The defensive lineman circled around Coach Mustaine and Darren. Jason stood next Darren.

Coach Mustaine led his group over to work on pass rush moves—initial moves and counter-moves. Up to that point, Jason's greatest pass-rushing weapon was speed. He wasn't built anything like Darren, and this fact left him liable to being pushed around in the running game. Jason would need to develop some counters to go along with his speed if he ever wanted to be anything more than a situational pass-rusher and reach his full potential as an every-down player.

A few reps into the drill, Coach Mustaine, already covered in sweat, jogged over to Darren.

"Can you take Jason off to the side and go through some counters with him?" Muscatine asked. "I think he could benefit from hearing your take."

Coach Mustaine looked maniacal with his face drenched in sweat. He wiped it down with a towel, and a loony smile curled onto his lips. Darren couldn't help but laugh and shake his head.

Coach Mustaine whistled. "Jason! Over here."

Jason ran over to Darren.

"You two get to it," Mustaine said before jogging back to the drill.

"A'ight," Darren said. "Get down in a stance."

Jason got down into a proper stance and looked up at Darren.

"Good job," Darren said. "Stand up."

Jason got out of his stance.

"After you use your speed on a tackle, he'll get used to it and adjust. He'll take a deeper set and get his hands on you quicker."

Darren put his left hand in Jason's chest. "That's when you hit him with a bull rush or rip move."

Jason's eyes were wide with concentration.

"Now, you're a little light in the ass for a bull rush, but I think you could rip just fine."

"What you mean, 'rip?'" Jason asked like the pup he was.

"When you're setting up a rip move, you wanna make sure you're rushing a third of the man."

"Huh?"

Darren put his left arm on Jason's chest again and simulated a pass rush. "See, if I'm pass-rushing you, I don't wanna attack you right down the middle because it limits what I can do. If you get your hands on me here—" Darren jabbed at Jason for him to put his hands up. He took Jason's hands and put them on his chest. "—there's nothing I can do."

They disengaged and Darren repositioned himself across from Jason's left shoulder.

"Now watch when I rush a third of a man," Darren said.

This time Darren came across and attacked the outside third of Jason's body. He put his left arm on Jason's left shoulder and ripped it down. Jason lost his balance, and Darren ran free to the make-believe quarterback in the make-believe backfield.

"You see that?" Darren said. "See how much easier it is when you rush a third of a man?"

Darren simulated this again, and Jason's eyes lit up with recognition.

"Okay, you try it on me. But be careful with my shoulder, hear?"

Jason lined up on Darren's left side and modeled the same action.

"You can go a little harder than *that*," Darren said.

Jason tried again and again.

"You came too far inside that last time," Darren said. "If you do that, the tackle can get his hands on you. Remember. Attack a third."

After a few more reps, Jason had it. He rushed the outside of Darren's left shoulder, and when he gained enough leverage, ripped down to free himself.

"There you go!" Darren said.

He raised his left hand into the air and Jason slapped it.

"Same thing'll work on the right side." Darren mimicked the action of ripping with his good arm. "I'll teach you some other moves before next week's game," he continued. "One countermove is good enough for the first game."

Coach Adams blew the whistle for the team to come up together at midfield. Jason ran over to the rest of the team, and Darren went to the sideline to grab a towel. His forehead was covered in sweat. He dabbed at it, and before he knew it the towel was soaked.

. . . .

Coach Adams ended practice fifteen minutes early and urged his team to go home, get rest and visualize a win in the first game of the season. Darren stood at the outer-edge of the circle next to Coach

Mustaine. Coach Adams did not address the off the field matter that was swirling around the team, mainly because he didn't know how things had turned out yet. He brought up the entire team, and it broke on "Sunnyside Pride!"—a cheesy slogan that Coach Adams loved, but everyone else associated with the squad detested.

Darren lingered after most of the guys hit the showers. Coach Adams looked at Darren sadly, not with judgement or disappointment in his eyes, just sadness, before joining his team in the locker room. Coach Mustaine patted Darren on the back and went inside as well. Darren looked down to the field, and for the first time, realized that he missed putting his hand in the dirt. That simple act, the one that every football player takes for granted, was the thing Darren missed most. When he lifted his eyes up, Marquis was there, standing by the entrance to the field. There was a potbellied, black man in a suit, lurking behind him as well. Darren walked over to his older brother.

"Marquis," Darren said "What's up? Who's he?" He nodded to the black man with a mustache.

"This is it," Marquis said.

"What?"

"I'm gone."

Darren looked at the man in the suit again. He knew. "But you weren't sloppy," Darren said. "You were never sloppy."

"None of that matters anymore. The past—all that. All that matters is what we do from this point on. Me. You. Mom. All these niggas in the Third Ward."

"Where you going?"

Marquis shrugged. A tear fell down the right side of his face. "I don't know. Someplace upstate. Maybe Leavenworth."

A tightness gripped Darren's chest, and the late afternoon sun beamed down on him like an interrogation.

"I don't want you to go," Darren said. "It was

good having you around. The way Mom was this morning. All that was good."

"I know. It felt good to me too. Just . . ."

Marquis reached out and hugged his little brother. He stopped crying. They squeezed each other tight, and the sun, the Third Ward, time—it all seemed to stand still. This moment was all that mattered. This embrace between the Taylor boys. Marquis pulled away reluctantly, not because of any static from Oatson—he was waiting patiently in the wings—but because it was getting to be too hard for him.

"I gotta go, little brother," Marquis said. "I can't be hangin' over you like I've been all these years. It's not fair to you."

"No."

"Tell Mom I love her. You're the man now. Try as hard as you can with her. Be patient. Don't be getting angry at her like I used to."

Darren nodded and his chest burned.

"And keep doing what you're doing out here at

practice. If you keep it up, you'll be playing at Boise State in the fall."

"Let me know where they're taking you," Darren said, breathless.

Marquis backed away. Oatson perked up because he too realized the electricity of the moment. Marquis remembered the pills and came forward again.

"If you ever have the urge to take those Oxys," Marquis said, "think of me. Think of why I did what I did. I gave it all up to make sure you get to where you need to be. Don't let me down. And if that ain't enough of a reason to stay away from the pills and stay off the streets, then think of Sadie."

Darren shook his head as if he heard wrong. "Sadie?"

"Yeah. Sadie. She's the one who's been cleaning up the mess I've been making all of these years."

Marquis looked at his little brother one last time. "Don't make any more mess for her, hear?"

Darren nodded and went numb. He couldn't hear a sound and the image of his brother walking away with the man in the suit was blurred, instantly swallowed by time. Darren blinked, and his eyes were focused again. Sound came back into the world. Marquis was gone. Darren's chest opened up. His head did not throb. There was a tap on his good shoulder. He turned and saw Jason standing there, smiling.

"Yo," Darren said.

"I don't want to bother you," Jason said.

Darren looked for Marquis one last time, but he was gone.

"You ain't bothering me," Darren said.

"Could you sleep the night before your first game on varsity?"

Darren remembered his first game on varsity when he too was a sophomore. Although the game itself was a hazy blur, he clearly remembered not being able to sleep the night before. A laugh caught in his throat.

"Sleep? Nah you won't be sleeping tonight. I wouldn't even try. Just go over your assignments instead, and eventually, you'll fall into that peaceful sleep. The kind you don't gotta try for."

"Yeah," Jason. "That's what's up. I'll just go over the playbook and dream about getting three sacks tomorrow night."

"You got the stance down," Darren said. "I'll give you that. But you better develop those countermoves before you think about getting three sacks in the game."

"I already got one countermove."

"Yeah?"

"Yeah, I'm ready to attack a third of a man tomorrow night."

"Good," Darren said, "That's real good."